"I've never met anyone like you, Sarah."

Craig extended his hand. She placed hers in it. He invaded her space, inhaled and smiled. "Your perfume. Meadow Romance."

"You remembered."

"Couldn't possibly forget."

Sarah stepped ahead of him, then turned and caught him appreciating the view. Her heart stuttered and his grin made her feel young. Pretty. She had no clue what to say or how to react.

Then she noticed the amazing smells wafting from the kitchen. "You're cooking? Really?"

"I said I would."

Despite her internal admonition, her heart leaped at his promise to spend time with her. She slanted him a quiet look. "If you cook, I'll clean."

"Promise?"

Craig's expression said he was two steps ahead of her in a game she'd never played. But she was beginning to like being on the board. "Promise."

Books by Ruth Logan Herne

Love Inspired

Winter's End
Waiting Out the Storm

RUTH LOGAN HERNE

Born into poverty, Ruth puts great stock in one of her favorite Ben Franklinisms: "Having been poor is no shame. Being ashamed of it is." With God-given appreciation for the amazing opportunities abounding in our land, Ruth finds simple gifts in the everyday blessings of smudge-faced small children, bright flowers, fresh baked goods, good friends, family, puppies and higher education. She believes a good woman should never fear dirt, snakes or spiders, all of which like to infest her aged farmhouse, necessitating a good pair of tongs for extracting the snakes, a flat-bottomed shoe for the spiders and the dirt....

Simply put, she's learned that some things aren't worth fretting about! If you laugh in the face of dust and love to talk about God, men, romance, great shoes and wonderful food, feel free to contact Ruth through her Web site at www.ruthloganherne.com.

Waiting Out the Storm
Ruth Logan Herne

Steeple
Hill®

Published by Steeple Hill Books™

STEEPLE HILL BOOKS

Steeple
Hill®

Recycling programs
for this product may
not exist in your area.

ISBN-13: 978-0-373-87611-2

WAITING OUT THE STORM

Suppose a brother or sister is without clothes
and daily food. If one of you says to him,
"Go, I wish you well; keep warm and well fed,"
but does nothing about his physical needs, what
good is it? In the same way, faith by itself, if it is
not accompanied by action, is dead.
—*James* 2:15–17

To my earthly favorite fisherman, my husband, Dave, who glimpsed the woman within the girl.... And married her anyway.

And to Helen Dunn and her family, whose lives were touched by sadness at a young age. If only there'd been an Aunt Sarah around back then. God bless you and keep you, Helen.

Acknowledgments:

Huge thanks to my children, whose help knows no bounds. Special thanks to Beth and Mandy for road-tripping the North Country with me, and huge thanks to Seth and Lacey for stepping into whatever job proved necessary. Matt, Karen, Zach and Luke... thanks for believing in me like you do, and special thanks to Sandra, Andrea, Tina, Audra, Glynna and Mary.

To Nancy A. Wood, of Wild Irish Rose Farms, a specialty farm producing goat milk soaps, and to Al and Rita Ostrander, proprietors of Ostrander's Bed and Breakfast. Thanks also to Mary Jarvis of Groveland Farm in Superior, Wisconsin for her love of Maremmas, to Kay Mott for her counsel on Native Americans and Nancy Vandivert, who offered advice on hand spinning.

Delighted thanks to Melissa Endlich of Steeple Hill Books for extracting the romance from the original manuscript, helping bring this story to fruition.

And always to the Seekers, women banded by love of God and romance, who put up with me every single day. You ladies rock!

Chapter One

Dr. Craig Macklin saw nothing but the massive creature before him, a huge, white and hairy Maremma guard dog beleaguered by a face full of porcupine quills. The obvious suffering in the dog's dark eyes implored Craig to help.

Craig squatted to examine the embedded bristles. The animal's curiosity had pushed him beyond caution. The face full of quills—a nasty lesson learned. Porcupines were best left alone.

Murmuring to the shaggy white canine, Craig positioned the adjustable light and peered into the Maremma's face. The dog's whimper made Craig's decision easy. "I'll have to put him under for a few minutes. The depth and quantity make it tough to handle without a tranquilizer. I'd be causing him a lot of pain otherwise. What's his name?" Turning, Craig looked at the owner for the first time.

Sarah Slocum.

Well. That explained Julie's initial hesitance, the concern he'd heard when his assistant summoned him. But his veterinary partner had left for the day and Craig was here. That left no choice but to treat Sarah's dog.

Her face washed pale under rich tones. Eyes as dark and deep as the dog's stayed trained on the beast's muzzle. She didn't make eye contact with Craig. "Gino. From Sofia's last litter." She emitted a half sigh, half shudder as the dog whined. She stepped forward, crooning, her melodic tone soothing the animal much as a mother would a small child.

Julie watched as if expecting him to do—what? Scream? Shout? Berate the woman before him for her genealogy and refuse to treat her dog?

He wouldn't do that. But his medical duties didn't mean he had to go out of his way to be nice, either.

There was a reason he avoided Slocums. A real good one. The thought of the criminal history between their families tightened Craig's jaw. Sarah's older brother had pioneered a Ponzi scheme, bilking a fair share of locals out of their hard-earned money, including his grandparents. Grams and Gramps Macklin had invested everything in Tom Slocum's guaranteed-returns package, and lost it all when Tom's misappropriation was discovered. Gramps had passed on over a year ago, but Grams was living out her later years dependent on others' kindness, with nothing but small Social Security checks to call her own. A tough old bird, Gramps used to call her, and he was right, but strong people have a hard time accepting handouts. Charity. Grams was no exception.

A true craven, Tom spared New York State the cost of a trial by taking his own life, leaving a wife and three young kids to sweep up the remnants of his actions.

Sarah had established a farm nearby. Goats? Sheep? Something wool-bearing, cleft-footed and ridiculously stupid. In Craig's estimation, the description applied unilaterally. Although he treated a wide range in a country animal practice, he'd developed favorites. Cattle. Horses. Dogs. Cats. Even pigs were a step up from sheep. At least pigs were intelligent. Sheep? Other end of the spectrum, entirely. No one in their right mind ate mutton, did they?

Hank Townsend, the senior veterinary partner, generally handled Sarah's veterinary needs, allowing Craig a wide berth. But he wasn't there, and Craig couldn't ignore the besieged dog. He glanced at Sarah. "You squeamish?" The question came out harsher than intended. A lot of people handled their own pain better than that of a loved one, including pets.

Julie stepped forward. "I can stay, Craig. I'll just call Glenn. He'll understand." Julie had a date tonight. Craig knew that because she'd chattered about it nonstop. Ralph, the other vet tech, had left over an hour before. And Maremmas…

Craig kept his gaze on Sarah, noting her lowered eyes. The dark sweep of lashes against honey-toned cheeks. High cheeks, at that, smooth and unblemished, not a freckle or mole in sight. "I know you'd stay, but Maremmas are singular creatures. They're bred to identify with their owner. They don't shift allegiance readily."

"I'll help."

Sarah's lack of inflection offered nothing. He eyed her, appraising, noting the air of capability belying her small size, then jerked his head toward the door. "Head out, Julie. We'll be fine."

"You're sure?" At his nod, Julie moved back. "Thanks, Craig. I owe you."

"No problem." Craig prepared the anesthetic as he spoke, studying the animal scale. "Ninety-six," he observed, glancing up.

Sarah nodded, jaw set.

Julie turned, then swung back. "Bagels in the morning?"

"With garden vegetables cream cheese."

"Can do." She shifted an uneasy glance from Craig to Sarah, then left, her footsteps soft against the tiled floor.

Turning full attention to the suffering dog, Craig bent. "Sorry, fella. I'll be quick."

As Craig administered the medication, Sarah eased small, capable hands down the dog's ruff, her tawny skin a contrast to the dog's white coat. She whispered to the dog, occasionally dropping her face to the thick fur, nuzzling. She seemed oblivious to Craig, which was probably best. Small talk options were limited.

Her family?

No.

His?

Ditto.

Her farm?

Not if he wanted to be anything construed as sociable. The finer points of sheep were lost on Craig, and lamb wasn't a dish his Irish mother offered except at Easter.

That left the weather. Or...

"Beautiful dog." Craig eyed the Maremma with a hint of envy, remembering his Lab's youth. Rocket was nearing fifteen now, slow to rise, and mostly deaf. Old age didn't go easy on big dogs, and his barrel-chested chocolate Lab with a graying muzzle was no exception.

"Yes."

She wasn't giving him much to work with, but maybe a quiet surgical intervention was better than empty words. Head bent, Craig snipped the quill ends with surgical scissors. Seeing her look of question, he explained, "Cutting the ends releases air pressure, making removal easier. Less painful."

"But he's under."

Her stoic tone caricatured Native Americans, her deep voice calm and unemotional. Craig nodded. "He wouldn't feel it now, but withdrawing the quills with the pressure would make the punctures more painful during recovery. The holes have to get larger to withdraw the spines if I don't cut them."

"Oh."

Silence stretched again, the passing seconds marking time from the old analog wall clock. *Tick. Tick. Tick.* "How old is Gino?"

Sarah's long, dark braid fell across her cheek as she soothed the dog. Her mother had been a Native American mix, Craig remembered, though he'd never met her. She'd died, when? Twelve years back, give or take. Long enough to have her self-absorbed stepsons grown and gone, while Sarah would have been a teenager.

At least Peg Slocum hadn't lived to feel the shame of Tom Jr.'s crimes. Craig thinned his lips, concentrating on the sensitive mouth of the Italian guard dog. The uncomfortable recovery could enervate the young dog, but he should be fine in the long run.

"Ten months. Nearly eleven."

Her answer took so long, Craig nearly forgot the question. "Did you rebreed his mother?"

"Next time."

"Must make it interesting during heat cycles." Craig eyed the dense mass of Gino and envisioned his sire. Substantial, like the son, and probably difficult to discourage when a nearby female was in heat.

"Neighbors take him."

"I see."

His cell phone vibrated. He glanced at the numerical page and bit back a twinge of guilt when Maggie James' number flashed in the small display.

He'd dated the local nurse several times over the winter, making her what? The third nurse he'd dated? Fourth, he realized. Amy, Kayla, Brianna and Maggie. Hadn't his buddy Marc joked that the hospital installed a new warning system designed to alert the female staff when he was on site?

Very funny.

He'd ended the short-lived relationship after the Maple Fest. What should have been a fun late-winter day had been relegated to shopping indoor craft booths because Maggie hadn't dressed warmly enough for the outdoor festival, more concerned with her outfit than the event.

Craig liked people. He embraced country life, the rigors of treating animals in all kinds of conditions. He felt equally at home in office or barn.

But not sheep barns.

Employing gentle twists and flicks, he withdrew the last barbs from the dog's muzzle, then stepped away to gather ointment and antibiotics. After glancing at his watch, he wrote instructions on a small prescription pad.

"You know how to administer pills to a dog?"

"Yes."

He handed Sarah the vial and the salve. "Apply the salve

twice a day. The pills are an antibiotic to prevent infection. Some of those quills went deep. You've got enough for ten days. If you see signs of infection or need a follow-up, give Hank a call."

They both understood the meaning of his words. Nodding, she sank her hand into the dog's ruff. "Come on, fella. Let's go."

"He'll be woozy. Might want to wait a few minutes, let him shake off the effects of the anesthetic." Regardless of the human awkwardness, the dog should have a few minutes of quiet, rejoin-the-world time. Walking the thick-set dog through the door, Sarah nodded, her chin tucked.

"We'll wait outside so you can close up." The weight of the dog listed her step. At the second entry she turned. "You stayed late," she said, her deep tone a blend of smooth gold and rough, gravel roads. A different sound, unique to her. A voice that suited her caramel skin, the long, thick braid, the high cheekbones that hinted at her Native American ancestry. She looked anywhere but at him. "Thank you."

He had no pleasantries to exchange with her. Nothing that wouldn't sound trite and manufactured. He huffed a breath as he shut and locked the door.

Minutes later he cruised out of the lot. Slowing his SUV to negotiate the turn, he noted the woman and dog in the cold front yard of the veterinary clinic.

Straight and still, she perched on the verdigris-armed bench outside the main entrance. The dog, equally quiet, sat upright, his chin angled with pride, mimicking her stance.

Maremmas. Great guard dogs, good bonders when housed with a flock at an early age. Smart. Independent. Faithful, not easily cowed. Willing to go their own way, awaiting no man's guidance.

As he observed the dignified profiles of dog and woman, Craig couldn't help but see how well they suited one another.

Chapter Two

Wherefore hidest thou thy face, and forgettest our affliction and our oppression? Sarah finished the words of the forty-fourth Psalm mentally, kneading Gino's ruff as he sloughed off his grogginess.

The poignant words touched her with their talk of sheep and oppression. Enemies. The poem was an aged song of lament and pathos. It helped smooth the dent to her self-worth, gouged deeper by Craig Macklin's disdain. How she wished…

Nope. She wouldn't go there. Refused to go there. Craig Macklin was entitled to his opinion, no matter how unreasonable it might be. Craig's reticence toward sheep was no secret among the local herders. The vets worked things out between them, leaving Hank the man to consult for sheep and goat problems.

By default, being a shepherd and a Slocum gave the younger veterinarian a two-fold reason to avoid Sarah, a task he did well. Knowing his grandmother's circumstance, Sarah understood why, but wished she didn't bear responsibility for her half brother's actions.

But she'd get nowhere feeling sorry for herself. No way, no how. She led Gino to the scarred pickup. The old Ford wasn't snazzy like Craig's polished 4X4, but it had a certain dignity in its aged finish, a little rough around the edges. *Like me,* she noted, shifting to allow Gino access.

The thought made her smile.

The memory of Craig's face erased it. The tall, handsome, sandy-haired vet usually steered clear of Sarah. At community functions he looked around her, avoiding eye contact. His animosity toward Slocums was unspoken but obvious.

She had never sought his help in a farm crisis. Today was an aberration.

Craig Macklin knew his stuff, though. In her years of farming, she'd never heard a complaint against him, and North Country farmers were not easily appeased. His thick, sturdy hands had been firm but gentle as he treated Gino.

She stopped by the local grocery before heading to her sister-in-law's home in Potsdam. Leaving Gino sleeping in the cab, she approached the front door.

No one answered her knock. She leaned on the bell with more force than should be necessary, if it were working.

Obviously not.

Unlocked, the door swung inward with ease. She stepped in, her nose telling her the whole place could use a thorough cleaning. Her eyes took time to adjust to the darkness Rita called home.

"Rita? It's Sarah. I've brought things."

No answer.

Sarah shifted the sacks and pushed through the antique swinging door between the rooms, its warm russet grain a comfort.

The kitchen was empty of people, but littered with debris.

Sarah grimaced, shifted piles of mail and old newspapers, then set the groceries on the table before she headed upstairs, calling Rita's name. A glance out the landing window showed Gino still asleep on the bench seat of the F-250. The driver's-side window was cracked open, but she didn't dare leave him long untended. A good dog, but young. He could get into mischief without direction.

Calling Rita's name once more, Sarah crossed the upstairs

hall and twisted the knob on her sister-in-law's room. "Reet? You sleeping?"

A slight movement revealed her sister-in-law's presence on the bed. Sarah stepped in, reached for the light, then rethought her choices. "I brought a few things. Where are the kids?"

"Movies. Liv took them."

"Nice. What did they go to see?"

Rita shifted, then rolled, a pillow clutched to her chest. "Some animated thing."

Sarah blinked. There was no animated movie playing in town. Did Liv take the car? Drive to Canton? She was two years shy of her license but she'd pulled some interesting deals recently. Sarah scanned the driveway through the nearby window. "Is the car in the garage?"

Rita's old-fashioned garage was behind the home, not visible from this angle.

"In the drive."

Sarah bit back words of recrimination. Obviously Liv had taken off with the car and the kids, with Rita clueless as to their whereabouts. *Dear Lord,* she prayed, trying to ignore the dank smell of despair. The room reeked of hopelessness. Loss of faith. A keen smell, the mix of body salts, sweat and sour breath.

"Come downstairs, Reet. I'll make us a quick supper." *Then I'll tackle my niece,* she promised silently, her anger rising. Couldn't Liv see her mother's desperation, the depression that seized her?

Of course she could. In her own adolescent way, Liv was trying to fill the shoes her parents vacated. The same thing that pushed Sarah to buy a farm on Waterman Hill instead of south of Albany like she'd planned. Rita and the kids needed sensible family around, and that was a scarce commodity in the North Country.

Sarah grasped Rita's hand. "Come on, Reet. Come down and talk to me; I'll straighten up the kitchen while we chat."

"Go away, Sarah."

The response brought Sarah's chin higher. "Won't work,

not with me. That's the one part of Slocum that bred true. I'm stubborn as an ox and you need to eat. Embrace the sunshine. It's almost spring, Rita. Let's go down together. Please?"

Rita clutched the pillow tighter. "I can't. I need to rest."

All you do is rest, thought Sarah, impatience rising. *That's all you've done for over a year.*

"You can. You have to. Liv, Brett and Skeeter are counting on you."

"Not anymore."

"Reet—"

"Sarah, I'm tired." Rita's gaze shifted to the curtained window. She blinked as if the shade-mellowed light hurt her eyes. "So tired."

The first months following Tom's death had seemed almost normal. Rita had gone on, looking neither right nor left, as if everything were okay.

But then the insurance company rejected Rita's claim because of a two-year "no suicide" clause. It had been eighteen months since Tom changed companies.

His smaller policy was intact, but the monetary value was minimal compared to the loss of his income. He had developed a retirement portfolio of stocks and mutual funds outside of his illicit investments, but they were inaccessible to Rita because Ed Slocum's name was included on the portfolio. Without Ed's blessing, the fund's worth remained out of reach until retirement. Twenty-plus years, give or take. And Ed had no intention of divesting the portfolio, regardless of Rita's financial situation.

Rita had crashed with that realization. Just slid right down into oblivion. Rita, who made eyes widen and mouths water with some of the most beautiful and innovative cakes and pastries the area had ever seen, now lived in a hovel, with ovens that hadn't been fired up since… Well, probably since the last time Sarah cooked a meal.

Watching the prone figure, Sarah felt overwhelmed. *How do I help her, God? How do I ease her out of the pain, out of the darkness?*

No answers came in the fetid room. Rita lay still, eyes open but unseeing, wrestling demons Sarah could only imagine. And had no desire to.

A scramble of feet and voices headed toward the kitchen a short time later. The door burst open. Gino, comfortably ensconced on the back porch, ambled to his feet, watchful and curious.

"Hey, Aunt Sarah!"

"Hey, yourself, Skeets. Come here." Arms wide, Sarah enfolded her youngest niece in a hug, then pressed raspberry kisses to the little girl's neck. The answering squeal and giggle was justified reward. "Gotcha."

"That ticklth." Skeeter's giggle displayed a gap in her teeth.

"They both fell out, huh?"

"Yeth. Brett says I look like a vampire." Augmenting the words, she bared her teeth and hissed.

"Oooooo… Brett's right. You're positively terrifying. How about setting the table for me?"

"Really? By myself?" Skeet's excitement quickened Sarah's heart. Such a little thing, to help a grown-up. Did Skeeter remember such things with her mother? The good times they had? Half her life had been clouded by her parents' choices. Olivia burst through the door, nose twitching at the smell of food. Brett followed.

"Something smells good. Hey, Gino." Approaching slowly, Brett let the dog give him a once-over, allowing space and time. Gino offered Brett a measured look, then a good sniff, ending in a typical Maremma token of acceptance. He licked Brett's face.

"Yuck." Livvie frowned, disgusted.

Brett grinned, accepting the dog's ministrations easily. "You're just jealous 'cause he likes me best."

"Yeah. Right. Hey, Aunt Sarah." Liv moved to the stove, her brows lifting in interest. "Smells great."

"Good." Sarah eyed her adolescent niece and stirred the

extra pot of gravy. Chicken and biscuits were a favorite, but biscuit topping robbed the gravy beneath. Extra was never a bad thing. Shifting her attention, she complimented Skeeter for setting the plates, then turned back to Liv. "What movie did you see?"

"Jinx, the Wonder Dog. It's about a dog that turns into a cartoon action hero."

"Really?"

Her tone put Liv on the defensive. "Yeah. Why?"

"Was it good?"

"It was really good," interjected Skeets, setting forks and knives in random fashion. Sarah re-directed her, showing her where each utensil belonged.

"How did you get there?"

"Drove." Opening the fridge, Liv pulled out a jug of juice and tipped some into one of the few clean glasses.

Sarah hiked a brow Liv's way as she set out a fresh green salad. "When did you get your license, Liv?"

"I didn't drive." Liv laughed, emphasizing the pronoun. "Shannon Connors did. She got her license in February. They moved into the old Rafferty house."

"She drove your mother's car?"

"Sure. Her parents both work and our car just sits here. Mom said it was okay," she added.

Sarah fought the sigh. No doubt Rita okayed the trip, then promptly forgot she'd given permission for someone to use her car. How long would it take two normal adolescents to realize the advantage they had when their one authority figure lay motionless, hour upon hour?

"She's a careful driver?"

Liv shrugged her dislike at being questioned. "We're alive, aren't we?"

Sarah changed the subject. "Supper will be ready in ten minutes. Anybody need help with homework?"

"I don't have any." Skeet's lack of teeth swirled the words together. Sarah smiled.

"Got mine done in study hall," Brett confirmed, his hand buried in the ruff of Gino's coat.

"How about you, Liv? Anything I can help you with?"

"For starters, you could stop playing mother." Her harsh tone brought Brett and Skeeter's heads up. They stared. "I'm tired of people showing up out of the blue, telling us what to do. We manage on our own."

Her anger reminded Sarah of herself at a similar age, her mother recently buried, her family divided. Oh, yeah, she had no trouble identifying with Olivia, but she wasn't big on placating mouthy teens. "Really? That's good to know. But it would be more convincing if the entire house didn't resemble a dump." Sarah cast a look around the kitchen. She'd made some headway. The dishwasher hummed, the counters were clear and the table set. The floor still needed scrubbing, but all in all, the room looked better.

Liv glared. "Maybe we have better things to do than clean up after her."

"You're mad that your mother's sick?"

"She's not sick, she's…" Liv hesitated, stumbling over words. "Lazy," she filled in. "Feeling sorry for herself. Look at this place." Liv waved her hands, half spinning, half pacing. "It's gross."

Sarah opened her mouth, but Liv kept ranting.

"Skeets wet the bed the other night and went to school smelling like pee. Mrs. Besset pulled me aside in the lunchroom and said the elementary school nurse wanted me to make sure Skeets takes a morning shower if she wets at night. I have to be at school at seven-fifteen," the girl expounded, staring at Sarah. "How am I supposed to make sure Skeets is up and clean for an eight o'clock bus when Brett and I leave an hour before?"

"Who puts Skeeter on the bus?"

"Mom. Or no one."

Groaning inwardly, Sarah figured the likelihood of no one. Skeeter's rapt expression said she understood too much. "Brett, can you take Skeeter into the living room while Liv and I finish up?"

"I want to hear the rest of the fight." He darted a look from his aunt to his sister.

"We're not fighting," Sarah corrected. "Your sister needs to vent. It's perfectly understandable."

"Don't patronize me." Liv stalked to the door and put the flat of her hand against the warm, cherry tones. Sarah was surprised to note the contrast, how pale Liv's skin had become. "You're not some social worker who thinks I'll work out my aggression by molding a lump of clay for thirty minutes a day. You're a sheep farmer. A smelly sheep farmer who wasted a good education to clean up animal crap." She pinched her nose to make her parting shot more pointed as she pushed through the door.

Ouch. Sarah said a silent prayer for patience, then one of gratitude for lack of available weaponry. Strangling one's niece because she insulted your pungent profession wouldn't sit well.

Definitely not worth it. Besides, who would watch the sheep?

She turned back to Brett and Skeeter. "Wash up, guys. Supper's ready."

Skeeter sidled up to her. "Aunt Sarah?"

"What, sweetcakes?" Sarah bent down, cradling Skeeter's cheeks in her hands.

"If Mommy never gets up, can we come live with you?"

Sarah's heart froze. Brett went still as well, his hands immobile beneath the water. Eyes down, he listened for her answer, just like his little sister.

Rita, get down here. See your children. Feast your eyes. Delight in the gifts of the Lord, your God.

No gentle footfall answered her prayer. No warm motherly presence brightened the dark corners of the room. Sarah pulled Skeeter in for a hug. "Farms do get stinky. Sheep aren't the freshest smelling animals I've ever met." Sharing a wink with

Skeeter, she rose and guided the little girl to the table. "But there's always room for you guys."

"Even if I wet the bed?"

Sarah made a mental note to buy protective mattress covers for the twin beds in the room adjoining hers.

"Everybody wets the bed when they're little," she comforted. Turning slightly, she noted Brett's stance. Silent. Still. "If your Mom needs extra help, of course you can stay with me."

"But you live in a different district." Brett turned, eyes wary. The faucet gurgled behind him.

"I can get you back and forth if need be, Brett. I promise."

Hopefully a promise she wouldn't need to keep. *Come on, Rita. Enough's enough. These guys need you. They've already lost one parent. Let's not make it two.*

Fear stabbed her. The look of Rita upstairs, clutching her pillow instead of her faith, seeking total solace. What would be more complete than to end it all, like Tom did? Unsure what to do, Sarah pushed down the frustration, made heavier by the events of the day. Gino's painful confrontation with a sharp-quilled beast, Craig Macklin's disdain and Rita's loss of control.

Shoving it all aside, Sarah drew a deep breath and mustered a smile. "Dinner's ready. Let's eat."

Chapter Three

The ginormous "Welcome to Doyletown" banner waved in the early spring breeze as Craig angled his SUV into a parking spot at the elementary school. Deceased for nearly a decade, Myra Doyle had created the Doyletown concept when Craig was a boy, and the Potsdam district continued the event in her honor. Children picked a pretend identity and profession, then approached a similar local professional to spend the day and talk about their work. Honored to be chosen by his nephew Kyle, Craig blinked back nostalgia as he approached the entrance.

He remembered his Doyletowns like they were yesterday, and having Kyle request his presence today?

Sweet.

He walked into the huge gymnasium and paused, taking in the spectacle of cardboard and balsa wood storefronts, the smell of kid paint and craft glue tunneling him back.

He grinned, caught Kyle's eye, waved and threaded his way through various exhibits.

"Uncle Craig!"

"I'm here, bud." Craig noogied the boy's head, laughed at the expected reaction, turned and looked straight into the chocolate-brown eyes of Sarah Slocum.

A waif of a girl clutched Sarah's fingers. The child eyed

Craig, wary, and slid further into Sarah's side. Her actions went beyond normal shyness, her gaze almost furtive, as if she'd rather be any other place in the world.

"I've assigned groups," the classroom teacher called out, drawing their collective attention. "Our class will do morning exhibit tours first, followed by lunch in the cafeteria, then professional presentations from our invited guests, then play time."

Talking briskly, she announced each group followed by six names. Kyle Macklin was followed in quick succession by Braden Lassiter, Glynna McGinnis, Jacob Wyatt, Carly Arend and Aleta Slocum.

Kyle groaned. "Not her. She smells."

"Kyle," Craig scolded, embarrassed. He turned, wishing he didn't have to, knowing he had no choice. "Apologize. Now."

Sarah's expression appraised him, one hand cradling the girl's dank hair, cuddling her, trying to assuage the hurt.

"Sorry."

Craig cringed inside. The sad awareness on the little girl's face broke his heart, regardless of her last name. Determined, he stepped forward and thrust out a hand, wishing he could undo the last three minutes. But if he possessed those powers he'd have hit reverse a long time ago and erased the adolescently stupid financial advice he'd given his grandfather a decade back. Maybe then...

Craig bit back a large ball of angst. There were no do-overs, unfortunately. Not in real life. The best he could do was set a better example for his nephew. He bent to the child's level. "Nice to meet you, Aleta."

She shrank back.

Determined, he stood and met Sarah's gaze. "Sarah."

"Dr. Macklin." Cool disdain colored her tone and Craig realized it looked like the apple didn't fall very far from the family tree, an assessment that bore some accuracy at the moment. Kyle grabbed his hand and tugged.

"It's almost our turn."

Chagrined, Craig dropped his gaze. "Kyle, you're being rude."

The boy's face crumpled, but Craig refused to cave. No time like the present to offer a show of good manners. He turned back toward Sarah. "Are you presenting today?"

"Yes."

"About?"

"Farming."

Duh.

She offered no help in the conversational court, but he deserved that. And more, no doubt. "Bring any sheep?" He swept the room a searching glance.

A ghost of a smile softened seal-brown eyes, the irises dusk-tinged. No hints of ivory or gold softened the deep tone, but the hinted smile brightened the depths from within.

Tiny laugh lines crinkled, then smoothed as she regained control. "I did."

Craig let his arched brow note their absence, then he bent low, catching Aleta's eye. "Do you see any sheep?"

A tiny grin eased the earlier discomfort. "No."

Craig slanted his gaze up to Sarah. "I think Bo Peep here has got herself a little bitty problem."

Aleta giggled. The laugh offered a glimpse of the pretty little girl hidden beneath a rumpled surface.

Sarah's expression softened, noting the girl's more relaxed countenance, but when she turned his way, her look flattened. "Live exhibits are penned out back."

"Ah."

The teacher's direction interrupted them and for the better part of an hour, Craig found himself on one side of the tour group while Sarah and her niece were on the other. Intentional on her part?

Most assuredly. Somehow he knew Sarah could command a situation as needed. Like any good strategist, she flanked the outer edges, skirting the perimeter, maintaining her distance.

Until lunchtime seating put them side by side.

Resigned, she stared at the small placard as if willing it to read something besides his name.

No such luck.

Craig pulled out her chair for her.

Her immediate reaction was half dismay, half surprise with a sprinkling of pleasure.

A very small sprinkling.

But it was a step in the right direction. After all, this young woman wasn't responsible for Grams' current circumstance, despite Sarah's family ties. And the fact that Tom's little girl sat alongside them, her innocent face shadowed by affairs beyond her control, piqued Craig's protective instincts.

"The wolf will live with the lamb, and a little child will lead them…" Snips of Isaiah's verse nudged Craig's conscience. No doubt he'd remember them better if he got to church more regularly, but on-call weekends interfered with all kinds of things, including church attendance. Hadn't his mother tweaked him about that very thing last week?

Aleta eyed the box lunch offered as part of the day's program. An instant frown morphed to a practiced pout. "I don't like this, Aunt Sarah."

"You don't even know what it is, Skeets," Sarah replied.

"I only like peanut butter and jelly and apple pancakes," Aleta whined.

"Have you looked in your box?"

"No."

"You might be surprised," Sarah noted. Opening hers, she pulled out a chicken salad sandwich. The little girl pretended to gag.

Sarah frowned. "Open your box and see what you have, please."

"PBJ" marked the top of Aleta's box, but Craig appreciated Sarah's attempt to encourage the child's independence. Scowling, she lifted the lid and peered inside. "Peanut butter and jelly!"

"Yes." Sarah pointed to the box top. "Those initials mean peanut butter and jelly."

"Why didn't you just tell me?" Aleta demanded.

Zing. Craig's protective instincts rose, surprising him. Why in the name of all that's good and holy would he want to protect Sarah from a six-year-old's onslaught?

And yet he did.

Sarah maintained a patient expression and tone. "You need to look beyond your feelings and see the things around you, Skeets. You make too many assumptions. Trying new things is good for you."

The kid didn't look like she bought the theory, but she stopped arguing long enough to eat, a concept Craig understood. Food ranked pretty high on his list of desirables, too.

Kyle chatted with Braden while they ate, a momentary peace established.

Craig should have known it was too good to be true.

Sarah sat alongside Skeeter on the bleachers, watching as various professionals fielded audience questions. People rambled in and out, picking which speakers intrigued them.

There was no small number of cute, female elementary school teachers in the room when Craig Macklin spoke. Surprise, surprise. They reacted like eighth-grade schoolgirls— exchanged looks, little giggles, smirks of appreciation.

Please. He was just a guy. A really cute guy, if Sarah was being completely honest with herself. With great hands, a firm jaw and a quick smile.

But that smile…

Too practiced, too glib, too smooth. Oh, Sarah was privy to the chick chat regarding Craig Macklin. Not only did the "doctor" title enhance his standing with the feminine contingent, his good looks and quick humor sent ripples of anticipation through a three-county area. But Sarah had been around long enough to recognize Craig's preferences. Fashion-doll pretty and dressed to kill. Since Sarah was a plain-Jane-in-barn-clothes girl, it mattered little. She'd take her small level of satisfaction in his more pleasant demeanor that morning and call it enough.

As Craig finished his spiel, Sarah's sheep were brought forward by two high school helpers. Sarah passed Craig without making eye contact, focusing on the two ewes and three lambs being herded into the circle's center. With the high school volunteers monitoring the sheep's antics, Sarah faced the audience.

"As you probably guessed, I work on a farm."

A chorus of "ohs" followed that statement.

Sarah nodded Craig's way as he retook his seat next to Kyle. "Because I work with animals all the time, I sometimes use veterinarians like Dr. Macklin to help me. Animals get sick, just like people and when they get sick, they need a special doctor. An animal doctor." Allowing a pause, she met Craig's eye in challenge, a silent reminder that he made himself singularly unavailable to sheep farmers in general and her in particular.

He squirmed.

She smiled.

"Sheep are wonderful creatures," she instructed, moving to the small flock. "They're dependable and docile. Very easy to manage. I brought two ewes, or 'mama' sheep, that just had babies. This sheep," she indicated the shorn ewe with a wave of her hand, "has been sheared. We shave their wool in the spring and sell the fleece to be made into thread for blankets and coats."

"People wear sheep?" asked a little boy, perplexed.

Sarah smiled his way. "Not with the animal attached," she promised. One of her teenage helpers hoisted an exhibit board while the other raised a blanket in one hand and a wool coat in the other. "Sheep products go beyond meat," Sarah explained.

"You…eat…them?" A middle-school girl's voice took a tone of pure, unmitigated disgust. "You actually eat your pets?"

A chorus of "eeeewwwwws" met her question.

The teacher reminded the group of hand-raising protocol, then shifted Sarah's way, awaiting an answer.

Sarah met the girl's gaze. "These sheep aren't pets," she

corrected. "Meat comes from animals. Every time you grab a chicken nugget, you're eating a bird. Hamburgers and steaks come from cows. Spare ribs and pork chops from pigs. And since protein is an important part of a daily diet, someone has to raise the meat you buy in the grocery store. I'm one of those people."

The girl looked freaked out, so Sarah switched her attention to the younger kids. "Baby sheep are called lambs. Aren't they cute?"

"Do you eat them, too?"

Obviously this girl wasn't about to give it up, and Sarah had no intention of lying. "Many cultures use lamb as food, yes."

The girl half stood. "You're kidding, right? You eat babies?"

Could this get worse?

Oh, yes. At that moment someone bent to drink from the water fountain at the back of the gym. The full-coated ewe heard the sound of running water and charged the fountain, eluding the teenager's hold and threading her way unceremoniously through the crowd. Pushing up, the ewe balanced on strong back legs while she licked the water basin, obviously thirsty.

Cameras clicked. Kids shrieked. Some parents laughed, some groaned, while others looked dismayed at sheep tongue fouling a water basin.

Pandemonium threatened until Craig Macklin crossed the room, commandeered the thirsty sheep by her collar and led her outside.

The circus scene squelched the rest of Sarah's presentation. Her antagonistic young questioner looked smug. Sarah swallowed the temptation to wipe the self-satisfied expression from the youngster's face, and realized she'd voiced what so many people felt.

As long as meat came without legs and a tail, modern society embraced the concept. Add a dose of reality? Big round eyes? Round wooly ears? Instant vegetarians.

Sarah didn't buy that mind-set, but now wasn't the time to weigh pros and cons of meat production. Embarrassed that she needed another rescue by Craig Macklin, she kissed Skeeter goodbye and herded the remaining sheep into the penned school yard, chin down, gaze straight. She didn't need to see the humor in his eyes to feed her mortification.

Ignoring everyone and everything, Sarah loaded the errant sheep into her scuffed-up animal trailer and headed home, eager for the peace and quiet of her small farm.

Chapter Four

Craig watched Sarah as she ably loaded the five sheep into the small animal trailer hitched to the back of her worn tan pickup truck, her head down, looking neither left nor right.

Her tight jaw and stiff hands were the only indicators of her inner feelings, but Craig had little difficulty reading the body language.

Downright mad.

But handling it well. Weighing choices, he considered offering help.

Her capable moves proved she didn't need it.

Or he could offer commiseration that would be unwelcome and more than a little in-your-face. Hadn't he professed the lack of intelligence in sheep loud and long?

No, he'd be the last person she'd want help from right now, and since she was just about set, he walked back into the gymnasium to rejoin Kyle for the last minutes of the day.

But he couldn't shove aside the look of her, the dusk-toned skin, big brown eyes, dark mass of hair threading down her back, softly arched brows. She had an earthy beauty that probably rarely saw makeup and didn't need it in any case. Breathing deeply, he remembered the scent of her at lunch, the soft, sweet smell of wildflowers on a summer's day, the sun shining warm on a field of heather.

But mostly he remembered her look of chagrin as the sheep charged the water fountain, a fairly smart move for a thirsty animal. He might have to rethink parts of his opinions on sheep. At least this one was smart enough to drink when thirsty. Didn't he know people who got dehydrated every summer because they weren't smart enough to grab a glass of water?

Today's situation had embarrassed Sarah and he felt bad about that, but there was little he could do. She'd mistrust his sympathy and reject his help if offered. He knew that.

Still, inner guilt rose because he didn't offer.

Kyle spotted him and charged forward, redrawing Craig's attention to the day's festivities. He glanced around for Aleta but didn't see her. Maybe just as well. Neither of those Slocum girls needed any more embarrassing moments.

Sarah cast a wistful glance around the warming room of her weathered bungalow and refused to sigh, despite the late hour. Most women would come home, stoke the fire, shower and go to bed. An appealing thought.

Her gaze fell on the dusty spinning wheel to the left of the wood stove, unused, untouched. She longed for peaceful evenings of spinning yarn, her fingers guiding the carded wool while her foot rocked the treadle. Someday there would be time for such pleasures again.

But first, the farm. Its success depended on her efforts. Long evenings spent crunching figures for area businesses left no time for spinning and knitting. She gave the wheel one last, long glance.

Someday.

Stoic, she left the inviting flames, donned farm boots and headed to the near barn. As she trudged across the drive, Gino kept pace, head up, attentive. Maremmas were great night guardians. Perfect for her, a shepherd alone. With them on guard, Sarah could actually sleep.

Mostly.

But lambing loomed. With the front barn full of soon-to-deliver ewes, a turn around the lambing quarters was essential. While she'd specifically chosen a Dorsett/Finn cross breed because of their less seasonal cycles, Sarah still engineered a strong spring lambing. Her January lambies were being marketed now for the Easter trade. This new batch would be sold in Albany and New York City come late spring and early summer, where eastern European immigrants celebrated love and marriage with roasted lamb, much as their Biblical forebears.

Sarah flicked the barn light switch then paused, her eyes adjusting, her ears tuned to out-of-sync noises.

All was calm.

Walking through, she found a new set of twins. The sloe-eyed ewe must have delivered late afternoon. Both babies strong and healthy, the caring mother uttered soft bleats of comfort to her offspring. The number of animals provided plenty of heat in this foremost barn, even in the bitter cold. Regardless of the calendar date, night temps could drop on the heels of a Canadian Clipper, a steep down surge of the jet stream. Tonight promised to be one of those. The wind blew intemperate, but the barn was snug. Secure. She'd made sure of that when she first considered this parcel. A cozy barn, good pastureland, large hayfields. Essentials to a northern shepherd on an accelerated breeding program.

And a house that needed cleaning. Cleaning she didn't have time or energy for most days. Satisfied with the scene before her, she retreated, closing the door with a firm hand, ready for a cleansing shower and a warm bed.

Baaaaaah.

Sarah turned, ears perked, drawing her coat closer.

A sharp wind chilled her neck. She eyed the dark field, knowing the next group of expectant mothers huddled in the second pasture. Not due for six to eight weeks, they should drop late-spring lambs that would be market-ready mid- to late summer, in time for the ethnic festival season in New York City.

As she turned back toward the house, the bleat sounded once more, followed by a bark, sharp and commanding.

Gritting her teeth, Sarah headed to the pickup, wondering why she ever thought sheep were cute.

Hours later, she was still unsure. The tiny lambs born in the cold meadow were taking their own sweet time to warm up. Sarah was sure she'd hit every rut in the farm lane as she traversed the pasture's edge in the pitch-black. An early-waxing crescent moon had dipped below the horizon long ago. Starlight did little to pierce the woods-edged fields and her long-handled flashlight kept blinking out.

She loaded the new family eventually, tempting the mother up the ramp by tucking the half-frozen triplets at the end of it. Then she prodded and prayed.

"It's a good thing Jesus liked you guys well enough to put you in His stories," she grumbled to the three newborns flanking the woodstove. At the moment, Sarah didn't find them all that appealing as she massaged the shoulder she'd wrenched during loading. She loved Christ's soft spot for shepherds, the parables and analogies. He kept it simple, and that worked for her. You couldn't get much more mundane than shepherds and fishermen.

Exhausted, she lounged her head against the worn cushion, the lambs snug in a garage sale playpen. Clutching an afghan to her chest, Sarah watched as the heat of the stove gradually chased the chill from the fragile bodies. Since the newborns needed to re-acclimate with their mother, she set the alarm for a two-hour nap, dozing with them, their quick-pace heartbeats offset by the strength and steadiness of hers.

The phone shrilled as Sarah adjusted the angle of the Pritchard teat to feed lamb number three the next morning. The others had rejoined Mama with little fuss, but the ewe butted this one away repeatedly. Frustrated and frantic, the hungry lamb needed food and reassurance. Frowning, Sarah let the machine pick up, knowing these first feedings were crucial. Hearing the message, she dropped the retrofitted soda bottle and snatched up the phone.

"This is Sarah."

"Sarah, it's Cade Macklin."

"I know. I heard your voice. I was busy with a newborn lamb." She inhaled nice and long, slowing her anxiety. "What's happened?"

"There's a petition regarding Rita and the kids. Someone turned her in for neglect. They want the children removed. Livvie's last prank opened a few eyes."

Liv and some friends had decorated the school superintendent's office with graphic posters when news broke that the administrator was cheating on his wife with the middle-school principal. Their little gambit caricatured the administrators with complex artwork, employing a parody on the superintendent's theme for the year: *Ethics in Education.* An eye-opener, for sure.

Oh, man. Where were these people when her sister-in-law needed help? When kids needed rides, or trips to the dentist? Nowhere to be found. But let a teenager step out of line and she was marked for life. At least if her last name was Slocum and she lived in a Podunk little...

Sarah choked down a sigh. "What happens now?"

"Social Services sent someone by Rita's, found it lacking in supervision, and will request the court place the children in foster care."

"Over my dead body."

Cade's voice deepened. "Can you take them? Judge Hicks won't grant guardianship to your father or Ed. Rita's people are in Albany, and you know how kids are about being moved around."

"Why are you doing this, Cade?" She didn't mean to sound blunt. Blame it on lack of sleep. Total surprise. The Macklin family owed the Slocums nothing. Zip. Zilch.

"Because Rita and those kids have suffered enough." The police chief's voice firmed. "They did nothing wrong, Sarah. Nor did you. And I can't see how sending those kids away will help a woman who's fighting depression. Maybe even suicidal."

Sarah thought quickly. "What about school? I'm not in their

district." Sarah's farm lay mostly in the Canton school district, although a small portion of her land crossed the border into Grasse Bend. Rita's house was north, in Potsdam.

"We can get that okayed by the board. They're good people. It might be tricky to arrange transportation for the next couple of days, but between the two districts it's doable in the long run. I'll work it out. That way the kids can finish the year in Potsdam. Maybe summer will be Rita's turning point. If summer ever gets here."

Since the winter had been cold and gray with little sun, the entire region would welcome warmth. Sarah agreed. "I'll do whatever it takes, Cade. This house isn't all that big, but I can stretch it."

"Good." Relief thickened his voice. "I'll talk to the case-worker and the child advocate. They'll probably come see you."

"Great." Sarah's living space longed for time and effort she didn't have right now, a touch she'd give it if she weren't constantly working on either sheep or business accounts or helping Rita. Her degree in business accounting kept her tending books at night for a growing number of local farms and small businesses, the steady funds helping her bottom line until the farm was better established. She breathed deep, contemplating. She'd started this enterprise willing to do whatever it took to make her farm successful.

Throw three disgruntled kids who disliked farms into the mix...

Ugh. She swallowed hard. "What should I do now?"

"Hold tight. I'll pass the word and have them get back to you. They're swamped, but a petition for removal is serious so it shouldn't be too long. Then the question is how do we help Rita?"

Sarah pictured her sister-in-law. Silent. Distant. Morose. "I don't know. I... She's...." Her voice tapered off.

"We'll figure it out." Cade's voice reassured. "No one wants to see Rita hurt. Or those kids. It's time for everyone to move on."

Cade's magnanimity seemed ironic when she'd been face-to-face with his brother's animosity too many times to count. Of course, he'd been nicer yesterday. Much nicer. Still… "Not everyone feels like you do."

"They will."

His assurance heartened her. The lamb, impatient, bleated an entreaty. Cade laughed. "Go feed your little friend, Sarah. I'll be in touch."

A small part of Sarah's heart loosened at this overture, the olive branch extended. "Thanks, Cade."

"You're welcome."

Sarah reached for the lamb. Angling the bottle, she mulled Cade's words.

Losing the children could push Rita over the edge and the fear of suicide worried Sarah. If they could get help for Rita while the kids stayed on the farm, that might help.

Liv wouldn't like this. She was a town girl. Her daddy had looked down his nose at farmers, and the girl took after him. That should be interesting.

Brett? A little uncertain, but definitely an easier-going personality. And he had an intrinsic love for nature, if not for sheep dung.

Both in the thick of puberty. Adolescence. Oh, man. An additional form of insanity right there.

And Skeeter. Skeeter needed someone to care for her, watch over her. Share in the joy of each new day when she wasn't whining or complaining about something, which was fairly often of late. Simple, by comparison.

But not one of them was accustomed to the sights, sounds and smells of a working farm.

St. Lawrence County boasted multiple classes of people. Those who farmed, including the Amish, their quaint wagons and roadside stands dotting a countryside thick with agriculture.

Then there was the upscale staff and alumni of Clarkson and St. Lawrence Universities. Throw SUNY Potsdam and Canton into the mix, and you had a diverse dynamic at odds with itself. Town kids might be raised within two miles of some of the best northern farmland in the U.S., but have little association with product or producer, fairly certain food came from the local grocer.

Sarah grimaced, remembering her family's expressions when she announced she was starting a farm.

They blamed her mother's Abenaki blood. The urge to be at peace with the land, one with the Spirit.

The aspersions to her mother's memory stung. Peg "Bent Willow" Slocum had been a good woman, a strong Christian who cherished her mix of heritages. Maybe if she'd lived, things would have been different.

But she hadn't and Sarah could pinpoint the day and time when she'd known where her own destiny lay. It was her first summer away, the end of her freshman year of college. She'd stayed in Cortland, working a sheep farm by day and waiting tables at night. She'd made enough money to guarantee her second year of studies and celebrate her freedom from the Slocum domain, the "me first" mind-set prevalent at old Tom's table. Her father was not a nice man.

She found the faith her mother inspired at a white clapboard church and a Bible passage that brought shepherds to a newborn babe, laid in a manger.

She found home.

Practicality insisted she finish her degree. A girl had to eat and farms weren't an easy venture.

Angling the bottle to keep the lamb from sucking air, a smile tugged Sarah's mouth as she regarded the tiny creature before her. Not easy, by any means. But worthwhile.

Chapter Five

Craig careened to a stop and pushed out of the car, instantly enamored of the view. "This is it."

His home site. He was sure of it. His new house would sit there, right there, at the apex of the hill, its south-facing windows benefiting from the winter's sun. Evergreens rose beyond the hill, close enough for privacy, far enough to let the winter sun shine unfettered. The slope angled toward the road in an easy climb, nothing too difficult for winter months. The adjoining land was farmed, but this parcel lay unplanted, ready for building. Native trees surrounded enough open land to offer fun. He pictured Rocket ambling through the woods, ears perked, hunting new sights and sounds. Maybe it would pep the old boy up, to have fresh grounds to explore.

Craig strode forward, oblivious to the weariness he'd felt moments before. He grabbed his cell and dialed Laraby Realty. "Steve? Craig Macklin. Listen, I'm staring at a piece of property on Waterman Hill. It's perfect. It lies between two farms. Across from another. Probably seven to ten acres I'm eyeing up. Yeah, that's right. The south side." Walking as he talked, Craig studied the site.

Home. He was home. He knew it the moment he rounded the bend. Now, depending on who owned the parcel—

Craig turned, his signal fading. "This is part of Ben Waters' land? I was at his place this morning, treating a cow."

Craig paused, listening. "I'll head there now." At the Realtor's caution, Craig shook his head. "I understand, but you know how old-timers are. If Ben's interested in selling, he'll be up front with me. Who's got the property on either side?"

To the west stretched old cornfields, stubbled and brown. Beneath the rise to the east lay a hay lot. Alfalfa. Across the street pastureland extended right from a barn adjacent to the road. He could see the peak of another building, back and behind. Left of the barn a small, dark house nestled among trees. The scent of wood smoke tweaked his nose, increasing the ambience. "I'm heading to the Waterses'. I'll call you after I've seen Ben."

Excited, Craig retraced his steps. Arcing a U-turn, he headed north. An hour later he emerged from Ben Waters' kitchen, stuffed with Etta's banana bread and the promise of a deal. Ben's handshake was aged but solid. "Have Laraby draw up the papers. I'd always thought little Ben would build there, but he's gotten used to the city."

Craig choked back a laugh. Little Ben was fifty-plus, and the city Ben referred to was the edge of Canton, off Route 11. Young Ben didn't have his father's farming instincts, but had made a good name for himself in investment circles. He'd orchestrated the retirement plans for half the county, both business and personal, doing well for his family. Things would have turned out quite different if Gramps had used Ben instead of Tom Slocum, but that was a useless complaint at this juncture.

"Thank you, sir." Craig clasped the offered hand, then surprised the old man with a hug. "I'm grateful. I love that piece of land."

"Well, now..." Old Ben scratched his chin, thoughtful. "I might hold out for another thousand or two if you've taken that kindly toward it." Craig's chagrined expression drew the old farmer's chuckle. "Gotcha. Tell your Realtor to come by with papers. I'll sign 'em. The building approval is up to date. I jes' kept renewing it, thinkin' it would pay off."

"I'll subcontract the work right away. That way I can finish the interior by the end of summer."

"I'm a good hand with plumbing," acknowledged Ben. "You need a hand laying pipe, I'll step in."

"Thank you, sir." Craig gazed into the worn, blue eyes of the smaller man. "I'll remember that."

"Congratulations, son." Jim Macklin clapped Craig on the back. "That's pretty country up there. And nice that it's a quick closing, no contingencies."

"Which means we can get things moving ASAP," Craig replied.

His mother seemed happy but unsurprised. "I prayed you'd find the right piece." She smiled as she handed him a hunk of fresh-baked bread, slathered with butter, her confidence that God had time for such little things amusing to Craig. "I asked God to provide everything you needed in a home site."

"Like God doesn't have better things to do than diddle with my building lot." Craig spoke around a bite of bread, then waved the chunk in appreciation. "This stuff's perfect. I was starved. I didn't stop for lunch and made do with cookies in the car."

"And coffee, I'd wager."

He grinned. "Long day. Longer yet," he noted, eyeing his watch. "I'm supposed to meet Marc at the park. We're running an eight-mile loop tonight."

"So showering now would be useless." She wrinkled her nose in his direction.

Craig laughed and frowned. "Sorry. I should have showered and gotten rid of the clothes before I came into the kitchen."

"That would be a switch." She nodded to the large kettle on the stove. "Can you shift half that pot into the eight-quart kettle for me, please? Dad's got a fishing crew on the *Deborah I* and they're due back. I want supper ready when they get here."

"Will do." As he poured half the soup into the smaller

kettle, he angled a brow his mother's way. "So. What did you ask God for?"

Her quick smile brightened gray-blue eyes. "The usual. Affordability. Hills, trees, land, good neighbors and room for dogs." She didn't mention Rocket by name. They both knew the inevitability of the old boy's future. Talking about it didn't make the outcome easier, although Craig hoped the Lab could make the move with him. Time would tell. "And I love that section of the county, so close to the state park. Beautiful land, Craig."

"It is."

"And it's a family home you're building."

"Yup. Me and Rocket."

At his name, Rocket almost perked an ear, but it was obviously too much effort. The misnamed hound let out a whine, passed gas, then stretched, his paws kneading air in his sleep.

"I was referring to the human variety, but…" His mother slanted a grin Rocket's way. "He's a solid beginning. Kind of."

"I don't think finding the right girl is as easy as you make out," Craig argued. "Can't say my luck's running any too good in that direction."

"Depends on where you're looking," she shot back. "Probably wouldn't hurt to expand your horizons, my boy. Search outside the box."

"Girls don't come boxed," Craig pointed out. "That would make things way too easy."

"Or Stepford," Deb replied. "When God puts the right woman before you, you'll know it. There'll be no doubts."

"None?"

"Nope."

"Like you and Dad?"

"Exactly like that," she agreed. "We've weathered some storms, but haven't capsized yet."

"And you knew right off the bat," Craig teased, grabbing

another slice of bread, then re-thinking the decision. Eight mile runs and full stomachs weren't a great mix.

"I was sixteen," Deb laughed, poking his arm. "But yes, Craig. I knew."

On his way upstairs to change into running shorts and shoes, Craig spotted Grams sitting on the side porch, a blanket drawn around her shoulders as the evening air cooled. He decided to drive fast and take a minute with her. Life had been crazy busy this spring and their shared moments had been few and far between.

"Grams?"

She smiled and turned. "Craig. I was just thinking what a beautiful day this was and now it's even better."

He grinned and sank into the rocker alongside hers. The wraparound porch, barren now, would teem with flowers once the nights warmed. His mother didn't care that most of their reservations were hunters and fishermen. She believed people should appreciate God, flowers and good food.

Grams leaned his way. "You've been busy, I hear."

"Crazy," he agreed. "And you?"

She laughed. "Your Aunt Cindy kept me hopping these past weeks. I helped when Lisa had her baby, and oh, my, that was a walk down memory lane." She patted his knee. "I remember you children being born like it was yesterday, your mom and I walking you and Cade through town in your strollers. Then on trikes. The idea that thirty-five years have passed..." she paused, staring outward, then gave a little jerk. "Anyway, it's nice to be part of this new generation. Watch you youngsters have babies of your own. Your grandpa would have loved that."

The wistful look in her eye magnified Craig's inner guilt. If Gramps hadn't died of a heart attack, he might be here to play with Lisa's baby. Or her little boy, Jack.

But no. Gramps was gone and hadn't known the joy of his great-grandchildren, except Kyle.

And whose fault is that, his conscience prodded.

Craig surged from the seat and noted the time, then hurried

off, unable to meet Grams' look, a mix of trust and loss. Would she hate him, knowing what he'd done? That he'd spurred the old man on?

Did it matter? He hated himself for the brash actions of youth, the foolish yammering of a young man who thought he knew so much.

He was living proof of the old adage his grandfather liked to quote: "Better to close your mouth and let people think you're stupid, than open it and prove them right."

If only he'd learned the lesson sooner.

Chapter Six

The first scream brought Craig's head up. It was followed by a second and a tirade of crude words Craig hadn't heard since party nights in college.

"I hate you! I really, really hate you! I'll kill you when I get my hands on you, you little worm!" The threat was followed by the slamming of a door, first once, then twice. As Craig hurried down the drive, a runner hurtled toward him, full tilt, arms pumping, an expression of half fear, half triumph lighting the boy's face.

Behind him pounded a girl, tall and lanky, her athletic prowess outstripping that of the huskier boy. Reaching out an arm, Craig caught the boy, noted the look of surprise and confusion, then held tight while the girl barreled toward them. "What's going on?"

"Let me go!" The boy struggled against Craig's grasp.

Craig tightened his grip. "Be quiet. Now." He directed a calm look to the agitated girl whose knowledge of words unsuited for God-fearing ears was most impressive. Keeping his eyes impassive, Craig stared her down. "Swearing isn't going to help your situation. I'm not turning him over to you until I know what he did to deserve the beating you can't wait to dish out."

The boy squirmed. Craig sent him a look meant to quell.

It did. Keeping his body between the antagonists, he angled his head. "What'd he do?"

"Besides reading my journal to his stupid friends over the phone? Even the most private parts?" The girl's pitch heightened significantly. With good reason, it seemed.

Craig squelched the boy with a stern expression. "Her journal? You would stoop that low?"

Trying to wriggle away, the boy realized the futility when Craig's arm clenched tighter. "It's just a stupid old diary."

"It's hers." Craig's tone allowed no leeway. "Private. Confidential. What were you thinking?" Staring into the boy's light eyes, he issued a challenge, man to man.

"I just wanted to see what girls write in those things." Reading Craig's expression, the boy turned sheepish.

"You've got a lot to learn about women, kid," noted Craig. He was about to continue when a swift-moving figure emerged from the far side of the barn. Startled, he recognized the tawny skin and raised planes of the cheekbones. Huge brown eyes, deep and dark, complementing the long, thick black braid. She'd obviously been working; she bore the look and scent of barn labor.

The girl rolled her eyes as Sarah approached. Then she sniffed, unimpressed, the sound insulting. The boy stilled as if ashamed.

"What's going on?" Sarah's voice held the same calm, flat intonation he'd come to know. Tilting her chin, she met Craig's eye. "You may let go."

"Of course." Irritation at being told what to do rose within him. "Now that I've saved his life, I'm expendable."

She didn't smile. Grim, she addressed the girl. "Who's watching Skeeter?"

The girl flinched. "She's watching cartoons."

Silent, Sarah didn't move. She used the full force of those dark, impenetrable eyes to subdue the teenager. Defeated, the girl fidgeted. "I'll see to her."

The teen flounced back to the small green house set in the trees, her posture indicating displeasure at life in general.

Sarah's gaze turned to the boy while the sound of a motor bore up the rise of the hill. As a group they moved the few steps to the road's edge, allowing room for the oncoming vehicle. "What have you done, Brett?"

Craig started at the name. Realization set in. Brett. Brett Slocum. Tom and Rita's son. The girl must be the older daughter. Thinking back, he remembered her from her father's funeral. She'd been in junior high then. Must be high school, now. Pretty name, too. Liddie? Tivvie? Something like that.

The approaching car drew abreast. Glancing up, Craig recognized Maggie James' polished silver coupe. She smiled and waved, then tooted the horn before she pulled ahead, angling her car to the side of the road.

Brett's look turned hopeful, maybe thinking his aunt wouldn't chastise him in front of others.

No such luck.

"Brett?"

He scuffed a toe into the scrabbled dirt along the road's edge. "I read her stupid book."

"Her book?" Sarah's exaggerated confusion flustered the kid. "She was upset because you read a book?"

"A journal," Craig supplied, keeping his countenance void of emotion with no small effort. Seeing the boy writhe under Sarah's surveillance brought back plenty of memories. Her interrogation tactics were not unlike his mother's.

Sarah's mouth dropped open. She gasped in righteous indignation. Her look implored the boy to set the record straight, declare the accusation untrue. Oh, yeah. Craig remembered the routine, front to back. Guilt 101. Did they teach that to women in class or was it intrinsic, inherent to the gender?

Brett's toe scuffed harder. Head down, he refused to face the look of disappointment on his aunt's face. Craig couldn't resist. "There's more."

Brett shot him an affronted look and jammed his hands into ragged pockets. Glancing from Craig to Brett, Sarah made no acknowledgement of the approaching woman, focusing on her nephew. "Tell me."

"I told Matt DeJoy what it said."

"You didn't." Her dismay increased exponentially. "You shared your sister's journal? Her private thoughts and dreams?"

The boy's toe dug faster as the charges compiled. His cheeks reddened. His shoulders twitched. He jerked his head. "It's just a stupid diary."

"There is no such thing." Sarah's tone dropped to the dangerously quiet level Craig remembered all too well. Oh, yeah. That tweaked a memory or two. Times a hundred, at least. He fought a smile as Maggie reached them.

With Maggie's intrusion, Sarah raised her gaze. Again Craig was struck by the unflappable expression. The lack of affect. He used to think her unfeeling. Unreachable.

Watching her interaction with the boy, he glimpsed the inner struggle. Saw the work it took to maintain the imperturbable appearance. She grasped the boy's shoulder, her grip unyielding. "Get changed. You can help me in the back barn. Five minutes." She added the last with a pointed look.

He marched off, defiant, much as his sister had done.

An awkward silence ensued. Maggie looked irked at Craig's lack of greeting and Sarah seemed ill at ease. She nodded his way. "Thank you."

That was it? He opened his mouth to say something trite, then paused, reading the look in her eyes.

Embarrassment. Shame.

The shadow was brief, no more than a glimpse, but evident. He nodded back. "You're welcome." Feeling out of his element, he turned to make introduction. "Maggie James, this is Sarah Slocum. My neighbor, it seems."

Sarah's look swept the work site cresting the hill. Something soulful flashed in her dark eyes. Pain? Her nod to the well-dressed taller woman was polite but swift. The tone of her cheeks went a deeper bronze. "I should get back to work."

Craig noticed Maggie's subtle appraisal of Sarah's appearance. Smells that clung. The dark flecks dotting her tall boots.

A protective surge swept him again. He fought it off. "Of course."

With another nod, Sarah pivoted and strode away, the set of her narrow shoulders rigid. Craig turned toward Maggie. "You came to see me?"

She swept his hillside setting a glance. "I heard you were building a house."

"You heard right. They just finished the fourteenth course of the basement. Not much to see yet, and probably not a good idea to hill-climb in those." He dropped his gaze to her spiky heels, about as different from Sarah's barn boots as you could get.

And why on earth that thought occurred to him was a wonder in itself.

"Probably not," she agreed. She hesitated, shifting her purse up. "You won't mind the smells out here?"

Craig crinkled his forehead, then relaxed. "You mean farm smells?"

"Yes."

He laughed. "Not at all. Especially not when farm visits are all in a day's work. I don't even notice it."

"I would." She sounded regretful, but resigned. "I just thought I'd stop by and wish you well with your building. I know it's something you've been looking forward to."

Forward to and then some. He'd had his house plans drawn up nearly three years back, then saved for the dream, living at home a year longer than originally planned.

Now his wish became reality, day by day, emergent from the adjacent hillside splendor.

And directly across from Sarah's sheep farm. How in the world had that happened when he'd been so careful? Thinking back, he remembered querying Steve Laraby about ownership of the land to either side of him. East. West.

Not across the street. He swallowed a groan with the realization.

As he swung Maggie's door wide, he mulled the situation. What were the odds that of all the acreage in the largest geographic county in New York State, Craig Macklin would end up building across from Sarah Slocum's farm?

What had his mother prayed for? Hills, trees, land, good neighbors and room for dogs.

The whole "good neighbor" thing presented a notable challenge. Craig's collar itched as he considered the situation. Every time he pulled out of his new driveway, Sarah's presence would remind him of things he'd like to forget.

Gramps' angst and dismay upon discovering their money gone, rifled by a scheming, two-faced investor. Grams' sadness. Their constant worry and guilt over being a burden, an elderly couple who had never burdened anyone all their lives.

That worry hadn't helped Gramps' struggle with heart disease. No sir. He'd died crushed and broken under the burden of decisions he thought fiscally sound.

Craig didn't need reminders, but here he was, building his dream home directly across from a Slocum. A band of them, if appearances could be trusted.

Craig massaged the bridge of his nose. If God had a hand in this, then he obviously had a sense of humor like Craig's father's. Dry. Subtle.

And not nearly as funny as he thought it to be.

"She's your neighbor?" Deb Macklin slid a wide tray of peanut butter cookies out of her convection oven, followed by another. Replacing them with two more, she raised a brow. "A sheep farm, right?"

"I guess."

"How big?"

Craig shrugged. "No idea. I didn't see the animals. Well..." He hesitated, reaching for a hot cookie. "I did meet the niece and the nephew trying to kill each other. I don't suppose that counts."

"Craig." His mother's tone scolded. "She took in all three kids because Rita's not doing well. I guess the money problems put her over the edge."

Her phrasing caught Craig's attention. "What money problems? The papers were full of Tom's private insurance and made multiple mentions of his other portfolios." He made no attempt to hide the scorn in his voice.

Deb shook her head as she set the oven timer. "They were wrong." She straightened and met Craig's gaze. "His major insurance policy refused the claim because of a suicide clause. His minor insurance paid, but that was a pittance compared to the cost of raising three kids. Keeping a home." She turned back to the counter and scooped rounded spoonfuls of cookie dough onto fresh baking sheets. "Tom's stock portfolio is tied in with his brother. Ed refuses to give Rita access to it. Rita sued for dispersal, but you know the courts. It'll be a long, drawn-out process. Ed's afraid his part will suffer if Rita withdraws Tom's share, and she's got no money to speak of without it. At least they've got medical insurance still. And Social Security survivor benefits."

"That's it? After all the papers said, I assumed Rita was swimming in cash. Free and easy, while other folks suffered."

Deb gave him a quiet look, not unlike the gaze Sarah Slocum leveled her errant nephew the day before. "You know what they say about assumptions, Craig."

He set his cookie down. "So the kids are living on the farm?"

"Yes. It was either that or foster care. Cade said Sarah wouldn't hear of it, though I can't imagine how she handles running the farm, her nighttime accounting business, and three kids. God love her, she's an ambitious little thing. When we needed sheep for the living Nativity scene last year, Sarah was the first one there and stayed the whole while, making sure everything went smoothly."

Craig hadn't made it to services that December weekend. A firm thwack of guilt smacked him upside the head. Was he really all that busy? Even on call, couldn't he set his phone to vibrate for the hour-long service and show up more regularly than he'd been lately?

Thinking back, Craig mentally scrutinized Sarah's face. Yeah, she looked tired. More, she looked determined. Stubborn. Intent on forging ahead. His mother's voice interrupted his reflection.

"You're not eating your cookie."

The oversized cookie sat on the counter, cool. Untouched. He shook his head, considering. "Not really hungry. I'll grab some for lunch tomorrow."

Deb nodded once more, intent on her task. "Whatever you say."

A slight sound stopped him as he moved to the door. He turned and frowned. His mother presented a calm, serene profile, not a smile in sight. But Craig had been her son a long time. He knew what he'd heard, her distinct low chuckle that said she found the whole thing humorous.

Huh. That made one of them.

Chapter Seven

Sarah considered the previous day's run-in with Craig Macklin as she aligned a fencing unit along the back hill.

Bad enough that Liv and Brett showed their worst sides, reinforcing current opinion of Slocums in general. But it had to be in front of Craig Macklin. Sheep-hating, sanctimonious…

Who was about to become her new neighbor.

Wonderful. No doubt he'd complain of the dogs' barking at night, the smells of a working farm by day. Sure, he was a vet, but he kept his visits to sheep country few and far between by design.

Recalling her appearance the day past, she couldn't blame him. Craig didn't come off as a guy who got his hands real dirty, regardless of profession. And his current girlfriend fit the profile to the max. Leggy, lithe and lovely.

Sarah tried to thwart a rise of insecurity, but it was no use. Feelings rose within her, how she prayed as a young girl to be normal, look normal, to fit in.

With Tom and Ed ragging on her constantly, she'd longed to be pretty. Attractive, like other girls.

Try as she might, though, nothing paled her deep-toned skin, softened the dense mass of hair or lightened her big, dark eyes. Owl eyes, Tom used to call them, then he'd make bug-eyed faces at Ed until they'd collapse in laughter at her expense.

Sarah scowled at the memory, kicked a raised piece of sod, and shoved the last fencing pole into place with more force than needed.

Standing next to Craig's latest squeeze, she had realized she had nowhere to go but up in the looks department, at least as far as Craig Macklin was concerned. And contemplating her planned showdown with her half brother and father, she didn't have the strength to care. Picking her battles had become a strategic necessity.

"Ain't none of your business, little girl."

Ed's words were typical Slocum. Her father used that phrase as well, a means to keep her in her place. It hadn't worked then, it wouldn't now. Sarah stood silent and patient, staring at Ed.

He twisted, uncomfortable. "Don't try your mother's tricks on me, squaw-girl. This is none of your affair."

Obviously Ed thought the word "squaw" insulting. Maybe she'd e-mail him some Abenaki history. Her squaw legacy was deep and fulfilling, a blessing for a woman of strength. Counting the longnecks on the table alongside his recliner, Sarah saw that Ed was on beer number five.

Great. He'd gotten an early start. Sarah continued to gaze at him, then angled her head. "I have three children who need their mother, one of whom is your godson. It would behoove you to act in their best interests instead of your own. You have no financial problems, Ed. You don't need that money. Why tie it up for Rita? What do you hope to gain?"

"You think talkin' like a highfalutin' college girl is gonna get you anywhere?" Ed blew out breath that smelled of sour mash and onions. "I may be simple, but I know my rights. Tom and I created that portfolio. Until a court makes me split it, it stays put. Rita can get her sorry butt out of bed and get a job. If she'd been more ambitious, Tommy wouldn't have had to take that money."

Sarah's heart hammered. Her lungs swelled. She wanted to smack him for insinuating Rita was responsible for Tom's illicit actions.

Instead she took a breath, a deep one. When the adrenaline rush eased, she brought calm eyes back to Ed's bloodshot gaze. "You realize you'll pay more this way, right? You could be held responsible for Rita's costs if the judge rules against you. As an accountant, I promise you it adds up quickly. Can you afford that?"

Ed belched and sneered. "Won't happen. Most judges around here are like me. They understand that one way of keeping a woman in her place is by controlling the purse strings. Want to know others?" He leered at her, his face suggestive, his gaping mouth showing tobacco-stained teeth.

She didn't act affronted. That would please him. To hear him talk like this, no one would know he was a businessman by day, successful in his own right.

"That's right." He nodded as she moved to leave. "Get back to your sheep dung and those kids you think so much of. I've got my own two to worry about."

Sarah strode to the car, chin up, jaw clenched, wondering why she'd tried.

Because it was the right thing to do, her conscience prodded. Integrity has its price.

But dealing with her remaining brother might be too big a price to pay. Ed's caustic sneers dredged up childhood feelings and fears that needed to be laid to rest. Sarah sighed, dropped her forehead to the steering wheel, and asked God to halt her tongue and bless her heart because as tough as Ed was, he didn't hold a candle to their father.

She thrust the truck into drive and headed to old Tom's, praying to keep her temper in check.

"Not my business, or yours," Old Tom scolded when she approached him, his forehead drawn. "You've got no call to interfere."

"I have three children who need a mother and shoes on their

feet," she replied. "Rita's beside herself with worry, Ed's a selfish lout and you have a responsibility to your grandchildren," she continued, striving to keep her voice level.

"Go against my remaining son to help the woman that pushed Tommy over the edge?" argued old Tom, indignant.

"That's untrue." Sarah maintained a calm voice, her expression staid.

"That longhouse mentality won't get you anywhere with me, little girl."

Little girl.

It had to be genetic. She fought the urge to tell him Abenakis never lived in longhouses. Like he'd care.

"Your mother taught you well," he continued, "but I have no intention of supporting Rita's drinking by giving her money. Ah…" Her father's voice hiked in a note of triumph. "You didn't know."

Sarah couldn't hide her surprise. "Rita doesn't drink." Saying it, she recognized her mistake. Alcohol and depression. One could so easily feed into the other. *Rita…*

"The kids know," her father insisted. "Olivia, anyway. She's the one who told me." He directed a hard look to Sarah. "You might want to be sure of your facts before you run your mouth."

Sarah met his eye, unflinching. "And maybe if Rita had the emotional and financial support of her extended family she wouldn't need alcohol."

"It ain't your affair. Or mine. I don't cotton to weak women and Rita's all that. If she gets her act together we'll talk again."

More punishment. Another twist of the blade embedded in Rita's reputation. Her lack of self-worth. Sarah faced her father, hands folded. Calm worked on her behalf before. "By that time you may not have the chance. Once Rita's better, she'd do well to shake the dust of Slocums from her feet, move forward and never look back. If you can't extend human kindness to your daughter-in-law and her children now, why would she want to maintain a relationship with you once she's healthy?"

"You're fooling yourself," Tom warned. "You see a strength that doesn't exist. Not in Rita, anyway. And she's no blood of mine."

"And those children?" Sarah eyed him, fingers taut. "Liv? Brett? Skeeter? You call yourself a grandfather and turn your back on them?"

"I raised my children, including you, and I wasn't a young man then, either. I've no call to be raising more."

"I see."

And she did. Clearly. Painfully. Fighting emotion, she bit back words of recrimination. They would do no good. Eyes down, she walked to the door.

Honor your father and your mother. The commandment rang in her memory.

She paused, considering, then left in silence, wondering if God considered percentages.

Hot tears stung her eyes as she climbed into the pickup. The night had chilled. Typical for northern springs. A promise of frost.

Sarah headed out of her father's drive, unsure if she'd ever come back. She had a Heavenly Father, ever-present, omniscient. Loving, caring.

What on earth did she need old Tom Slocum for? Straining her brain, nothing much came to mind on that cold, dark ride home.

Visiting Rita's the next afternoon, Sarah noticed the sharp tang of whiskey, used and unused.

How had she missed it? Was Rita less worried about hiding it with the kids gone?

Eyeing the mess, Sarah shook her head, then prayed. *Help me, Father. Stay with me. I'm in over my head and haven't the vaguest idea how to help.*

What do I say to her? What will it take to jerk her out of this rut? I'm not smart enough to see the answers. If You've got 'em, share 'em, because I'm fresh out of ideas.

Rita sat on the back porch, staring at nothing. She jerked when Sarah stepped out, her hand flying to the glass alongside.

Clumsy, her hand slipped and the glass flew, shattering on the cracked tile floor.

Rita swore. In fifteen years of knowing her, Sarah had never heard Rita utter a profanity.

Now angry and upset, obviously worried that Sarah might find her out, she sputtered words to impress a land-locked sailor.

"Stop it." Sarah grabbed her hands, tugging her back. "You'll cut yourself."

"I have to clean this up. The kids are coming."

Pulling harder, Sarah hauled Rita away from the mess. "They're not."

Rita paused in her struggle. Her fair hair, once lustrous, lay dank and dull. The blond shade, not passed to any of her children, carried glints of silver that used to look like she'd paid good money for ash-blond highlights. Rita liked to say the effect was a combination of her and God. Nothing over-the-counter.

She was in desperate need of shampoo and conditioner. Plenty of both.

The stench of unwashed skin and Black Velvet filled the porch despite open windows and a sweet spring breeze. Sarah guessed Rita hadn't changed clothes in days, her top flecked with faded stains.

Her face appeared haggard, the eyes despondent, with bags beneath. She was thirty-six years old and looked fifty. And that was generous.

Sarah stood quiet, overwhelmed. She'd put in a long week already, the change of seasons forcing necessary fieldwork. She'd rotated ewes, fed stock that wasn't on pasture, docked tails and inoculated lambs, cleaned the barn, tended dogs and pups, prepared meals, worked accounts at night, and minded three children, two of whom resented everything she represented. Now she faced a drunken, depressed sister-in-law with a death wish.

In a total tactical reversal, Sarah went on the offensive.

"Why are you doing this?" she demanded. Dismay flickered

across her sister-in-law's face, but Sarah let it slide, for once not shielding her emotions. "You've got three beautiful children and the rest of your life ahead of you. Who cares about my brother? Get over it, already. I'm tired of everything in our lives dating from Tom's death. Right now I hate him, and I'm not all that fond of you."

"You sound like Livvie."

A wry note colored Rita's voice, but Sarah was on a roll. "Well then, the girl's got more common sense than her mother. At least she gets her feelings out and moves on rather than shutting herself up, drinking herself to death. Is that what these kids need? Another suicide? Because that's where you're headed, Reet."

Rita's face paled.

Sarah pushed harder. "I dread the day I walk in here and find you dead from alcohol or depression. And I'm tired of it," Sarah continued. "What's gotten into you? Can't you see the beauty around you? The stars, the trees? Don't you know they'll all be here, watching and guarding long after you and I are dead and gone? Praise God, girl, there is beauty everywhere you look if you'd just open your eyes. Drink it in. Instead of the eighty-proof stuff you've pickled yourself with." Sarah pounded her fist once more before noting the hopeless expression on Rita's face. With effort she softened her tone.

"I need you. The kids need you. But I can't take this any more. Coming over here, seeing you like this. I go home and all I do is worry about you. Pray for you. Beg God for help so I know what to do. But I haven't got a clue. I don't know how to help you on top of everything else I'm supposed to handle. The farm. The kids. The accounts. The house." That last brought a groan as Sarah realized the state her own house was in. Before she'd left she'd made a list for Brett and Liv, threatening their extinction if it wasn't carried out. If they shrugged it off, that would be another confrontation, and frankly, she was tired of butting heads. She drew a breath and turned her attention back to Rita.

"I'm through playing games. When I walk out this door,

I won't be back. Not until you've made steps toward getting better. All the mental health visits in the world will be for nothing if you wallow in whiskey." She leaned against the door, her heart heavy. "The ball's in your court, Reet. I've got your kids, and I have no intention of letting their last memories of their beautiful mother be this." She waved a hand, including Rita and the porch clutter. "It's the booze or the kids. There is no third choice."

Rita sat, impassive. She stared beyond Sarah, eyeing nothing, lips pressed together, hands clutching the arms of the deck chair. Sarah watched, waiting, but Rita made no move. After long moments, Sarah turned. Quiet, she made her way through the kitchen and the hall, past the living room that smelled of decaying fruit and mildewed sneakers. Reaching the front door, she turned the handle with more force than necessary, bit her lip and yanked, fighting the urge to slam it in her wake.

"Sarah."

Sarah almost didn't hear the voice, a spoken whisper, faint and feathered.

"Sarah. Please."

She turned. Rita stood in the arch of the russet door, one hand extended. "Help me. Please."

Sarah hesitated, gripping the knob. Rita blinked. Drew a breath. "Please."

Sarah stayed planted, her fingers clamped around the smooth, gold handle. "I'm not messing around, Rita."

"I know." Rita took a short, ragged breath, then nodded. "Neither am I."

"No more drinking? You'll join AA?"

Another breath widened Rita's eyes. Sarah wasn't sure if it was the idea of going public or the infusion of non-alcohol laced oxygen to her bloodstream. While AA was labeled "anonymous", everyone in Potsdam knew why you were headed in or out of St. Luke's basement on Tuesday nights, the downside of small town living. Rita hesitated, then dipped her chin, decisive. "Yes."

She came forward. Reaching out both hands, she moved toward Sarah. "I'm scared. So scared."

Releasing the door, Sarah closed the distance between them. "Of what?"

"Everything."

Nothing vague about that. Sarah drew a deep breath. "One day at a time, Reet. That's all I ask."

"I don't know what to do about money. The bills. How to provide for the kids."

"Doesn't God provide for the sparrows of the air? How much more worthy are you than a bird? He'll take care of us, Rita." She emphasized "us." "You're not alone."

"There's so much," murmured Rita, her glance taking in the condition of the house. Fluttering hands indicated her appearance. Ragged. Slovenly. "I don't know where to start."

"You just did." Hugging her, Sarah patted her back much as she would Skeeter's. "I'll call Dr. Roth. Get things moving."

"No." Rita took a deep breath and reached for the phone. "I need to do it."

Even better.

Sarah moved back. "I'll be in the kitchen."

Chapter Eight

"She's a drunk," Liv acknowledged, flat and sharp.

"An alcoholic," Sarah corrected.

"A skunk by any other name still smells like a skunk," Liv shot back. Her eyes flashed disgust. She spun, ready to leave the room.

"Don't move, Liv," Sarah warned. "We've got things to discuss."

"Will she live in the hospital?" Brett asked.

"Just for two weeks. They have a special program, but it's not like your mom has to stay. She stays because she makes the decision to do it each day. And she'll join Alcoholics Anonymous."

"What's that?" asked Brett.

"Drunks-R-Us," retorted Liv.

Brett scowled at Livvie. "I don't think it's nice to make fun of Mom."

"I agree," Sarah told him. "But Liv has a right to be mad with all that's gone on. She's had to shoulder a lot of responsibility these last two years, and that's not easy." Lifting her shoulders, she shrugged. "I wish I could tell you it's all over. That everything will be better." She reached out a hand and tousled Brett's hair. "I can't do that. But I think we're on the right track."

"What if she starts drinking again?"

Sarah refused to make false promises. These kids needed assurance and honesty, two things they hadn't experienced for a long time. "Then we start again. But we're going to pray that doesn't happen."

Sarah saw the lesson for the two-edged sword it was. Openness meant the opportunity for Rita to get well. Conquer her dragons.

It also meant public knowledge. Kids knowing Livvie's mother was a member of AA, one of those close-lipped secrets everyone knew. It wasn't enough that their father bilked money from innocent people then hung himself upon discovery. Oh, no. Toss a drunken, depressive mother into the mix and see how popular the Slocums were.

Sarah pushed away from the table. "You guys did okay with the housework while I was gone. Thanks for seeing to it. I've got to take care of some things in the barn. Who wants to help me and who wants to watch Skeet?"

Silence met her words, then Brett jerked a shoulder. "I'll help you. I checked on Molly earlier. Nothing yet."

"Thanks for doing that." Sarah smiled her appreciation. Molly was her soon-to-deliver Border collie. A wonderful dog. They'd made a nesting stall for her at the opposite end of the barn from Lili, the Maremma with the current litter. Under normal circumstances the dogs got on well, but new mothers were unpredictable. "We'll check her again when we're done outside."

Brett nodded. Sarah eyed Liv. "Pizza for supper?" The idea of cooking after barn work held little appeal.

"In town?"

Saying yes would push Sarah's evening work late, but Liv's hopeful note made her decision easy. "That's a great idea. You and Skeeter get cleaned up while Brett and I do chores, then we won't have to fight for bathroom space. Deal?"

"Yup."

"Liv, will you do my hair? Make it pretty?" Skeet's voice danced with excitement.

"Sure. And we can listen to Taylor Swift full blast."

Sarah grinned at Brett's look. He might appreciate the young superstar's other attributes but couldn't get into lyrics that spouted the attributes of Romeo and Juliet. Romantic he wasn't, and just as well at this age.

Liv and Skeeter knew the songs verbatim and thought nothing of letting them fly at the top of their lungs.

Marc DeHollander's red Herefords complemented the spring green of his broad upper pasture. Shaggy ivory heads sat proud atop thickset, ruddy forms, a great contrast against the thick new grass they foraged. "Looking good, Marc," Craig noted to his friend. A third-generation farmer, Marc had branched into beef cattle. His years of hard work were finally paying off. "Everything's up to date. When the new bull arrives, give me a call. We'll give him a once-over."

"He's a beauty," Marc responded, latching the gate. "Brings Diamond Back bloodlines into the group. Stocky form, quick growth, easy birthing."

"Every cow's dream." Craig grinned and clapped the other man on the back. "How's your dad?"

Marc's expression tightened. "All right. The treatment's pretty rough, and the long-term prognosis is iffy, but he's tough. He'll be okay." The shadow in his eyes belied his optimism.

Craig took the words at face value. "Good."

Pete DeHollander was a fine man. A good farmer. Moreover, he was a strong proponent of change, not always a welcome thing among old-time farmers. Craig had been saddened by the news of his cancer. "Give him my best."

"I'll do that. How's the house coming? You tired of sheep yet?"

Craig laughed. The idea that he'd found his home site in the middle of sheep country amused Marc no end. "Not yet. I've moved my parents' camper on-site and hooked into the electric lines so I can stay there, but work's been busy."

"Pays the bills." Marc eyed the SUV. "Nice wheels. Babe magnet."

Craig swiped a finger across the pervasive coating of farm dust. "Yeah. Beating them off with a stick."

"Well, one anyway. The nurse. The current nurse, that is."

Craig made a face. "Overzealous."

"Because you messed with the three-date maximum," Marc noted. "It's your own fault."

They had connived a formula during a fairly long night at a local country and western hangout years before. Unless your intentions included a gold band, three dates was the max. By the fourth date, women were imagining veils, envisioning nurseries. It wouldn't do to leave a trail of broken hearts in the North Country. If there was no ever-after spark by date three, the warning knell sounded. Craig frowned. "You're right. Somewhere in that cockeyed formula lay a glimmer of common sense."

"Which is amazing, considering how long we hung out that night."

Craig grinned. "True. I distinctly remember dancing to ABBA at one point."

"Fearsome memory right there," Marc noted. "ABBA or a pack of hungry wolves?" Marc offered the choice in jest, an old comparison game they'd devised as boys. Most everything paled in comparison to a pack of hungry wolves.

But not always.

"The wolves. Definitely." Craig tapped a finger along the fence rail. "Unless I'm totally over the top and the girl's got long, blond hair."

"Factors affect outcome." Marc shot him a knowing look. "Perfectly understandable. But you deserve whatever you get, Macklin, for dating women who'll never make it in farm country."

"Some of them could be adaptable," Craig argued. "You might want to broaden your horizons yourself, old man."

"You're kidding, right? When and if I get serious, I want someone who works with the farm, not against it. Marriage is tough enough without increasing the odds of failure by ignoring the obvious."

Craig contemplated that, remembering Marc's mother. Her exodus from the farm and her family. How rough that was for the DeHollanders, dealing with the gossip and speculation. "True enough."

"And with your new convenient location, you might not be able to pass as many sheep duties on to Hank."

"Which amuses Hank, of course." Craig's tone said it was anything but amusing.

Marc grinned, then arched a brow. "You near Sarah Slocum?"

Craig's internal radar hiked up. His shoulders tightened. "Across the street. Why?"

Marc shrugged, easy. "No reason. I was just surprised she set up here. There wasn't much love lost between the older Slocums and Sarah. Tom and Ed gave Sarah a real tough time when she was a kid."

Craig's adrenalin surge pumped higher. "She's their sister."

"Not on Slocum terms. I don't have to fill you in on their mind-sets, do I? Look at the girl."

Craig envisioned Sarah. Small, latte-toned. Huge, expressive eyes. Thick, blue-black hair braided against her head. For just a moment he wondered what it would look like without the braid, the thick fall of hair tumbling around narrow shoulders. Her small waist. What would it feel like, the weight of her hair in his hands?

"Not exactly their version of all-American," Marc continued, interrupting Craig's thoughts. He blew out a breath. "They made her life rough. I didn't think she'd ever come back, much less settle here."

"How well do you know her?"

"A bit. I was two years ahead of her in college. We had a business law class together. Did some studying." Marc shifted his weight, remembering. "She's quiet, but she shared enough for me to see she was different from the rest. And to realize what growing up with Tom and Ed must have been like."

Pushing off the fence, Craig pondered Marc's words. What kind of family acted like that? Not his, certainly. He turned to Marc and stuck out his hand. "Call me when your new investment arrives. I'm anxious to view the future of DeHollander Hereford Holdings."

Marc grinned his pride at the direction his venture was taking. "Me, too."

Appointments done, Craig pulled into the municipal parking lot of Grasse Bend. Cade's police office anchored the west side, offering a good view of the town center and passersby.

A street of shops bordered the eastern edge. Craig swung open the door to North Country Woodcrafters, the entry bell announcing his presence. Brooks Harriman raised his chin and smiled a welcome. "Afternoon, Doc."

Craig grinned. "Hey, Brooks. Thought I'd see you about some furniture."

"Your place is coming along?"

"Yes." Craig ran his hand along the level planes of a corner cupboard. The wood felt cool despite the afternoon sun. "I like things that look strong. The house is post and beam, so it's got a country feel."

Brooks inclined his head. "Which room are we talking? Living room? Kitchen? Bedroom?"

"Bedroom first. Nineteen by sixteen. Southern and western exposures, third level."

"Good view?"

Craig laughed. "Once the windows are cut in."

"Sloped ceilings?"

"Not in this room."

"It can handle something substantial."

"Yes."

Brooks motioned Craig to follow him. "I've got headboards and footboards out here. Generally the bed dominates the master bedroom and the dressers accent that. My advice would be to pick a bed style that suits; we'll create furniture to match it."

Could it be that easy? Inspecting the samples in the elongated showroom, Craig's attention was caught by a northwoods display. "That's it."

"The northern white cedar?" Brooks eyed the Adirondack-style bedstead. "That would work."

"It's perfect," noted Craig, running his hand over the smoothed logs. "Rough and rustic."

"Male."

Craig grinned. "Yeah. Can we stain it darker?"

"Of course. You might want to consider—" The entry bell cut Brooks short. Both men looked up. Maggie stepped down and moved toward them.

"I thought that was your SUV out there," she bubbled to Craig. "Cade said he hadn't seen you, so…" She laughed and shrugged. "I came here. Looking at furniture?"

Craig's collar tightened. His palms itched. "Thought I'd nose around. See what worked." He carefully didn't ask her opinion.

She gave it anyway. "Wouldn't this cherry look good? Cherry has such an old world grace." She traced the tapered edges beneath her fingers. "How nice that would be if you did the kitchen in cherry as well. Don't you think so, Mr. Harriman?"

Brooks cleared his throat. "Cherry's nice."

Craig shot him a "what are you thinking?" look. Brooks grinned.

"I'm partial to oak and hickory," admitted Craig. "Deeper grains."

"But oak's sooo overdone," the young woman observed. "Oak this, oak that. Like there wasn't any other kind of tree. Please. Cherry has a certain ambience. It says class without being ostentatious."

Craig bit back a retort and sidestepped the issue. "It's hard to make a decision with the house unfinished. And something I'm going to have to live with better be well-thought."

"I agree," interjected Brooks. "It pays a man to know the difference between veneer and solid wood. What lasts in the long run."

Craig had no trouble understanding the double entendre. He faced Brooks. "You're right. Veneer's got its place, but I'm a hardwood kind of guy."

"Post and beam does that to a man."

Maggie glanced from one to the other. "That's still hardwood, right?"

Craig eased toward the door. "Brooks, thanks for the help."

"Anytime, Doc."

Outside, Maggie hugged herself, warding off the late-afternoon chill. "It was so warm in there." She eyed Brooks' window, filled with rustic offerings to tempt potential buyers. Lodge stuff, total northwoods. A sure draw to the northern traveler.

Determined not to lead her on, Craig opened Maggie's car door for her, waited as she climbed in, then offered a brief goodbye.

Climbing into the SUV, he pondered Brooks' words. *"It pays a man to know the difference between veneer and solid wood."*

Wood said a lot about a person. He wasn't surprised that God picked a carpenter to raise his son. Teach him the trade. Many lessons could be learned at the lathe.

Climbing the cinder drive, Craig recalled his mother's words. *It's a family house, Craig.*

Craig eyed the imposing framework. Would he rattle around this beautiful home, its space mocking him, underscoring his solitude? Even if Rocket came along, the old guy spent most of his days sleeping. Considering the dog's age, Craig knew their time was limited.

"I will lie down and sleep in peace, for you alone, O Lord, make me dwell in safety." The comforting words of the fourth Psalm ran through his mind.

In God's time. That's what his mother would say. Craig eyed the clean, strong lines of the rising structure.

He knew better than to rush things. His parents' counsel on matters of faith was ingrained. He had no trouble believing in the Master's plan, a Heavenly framework, but he wasn't foolish enough to think God weighed the picayune needs of every man, woman and child. Even God had to draw the line.

Surveying the beautiful home, he felt dwarfed by the proportions. "What was I thinking?" he muttered as he trudged to the camper, the skeletal house looming huge and empty.

He had no idea.

Chapter Nine

Herding the kids toward the side doors of the quaint, old church, Sarah spotted Craig's rangy frame. He was talking with someone, bent to allow for the height difference. Walking past, she sent him another quick look, only to meet those amber eyes head on.

He smiled. Inclined his head, just a little.

Her heart quickened. It was a boyish grin, a mix of mischief and innocence.

Stiffening, she straightened her shoulders, shifted her gaze and made it to the door without looking back, wondering why she looked in the first place.

She almost smiled.

Talk about incongruous. He was happy because Sarah Slocum nearly smiled at him. What had gotten into him?

Spring fever, he decided, making his way to the exit. He clasped Rev. Weilers' hand. "Great homily, sir. I needed that reminder."

The reverend shook Craig's hand and dropped a wizened wink. "Come more often, Doc. I dole out reminders on a regular basis." Grinning at Craig's discomfiture, he made a quick change of subject. "So. You found Tippy in good health."

Craig hedged. The reverend's dog was nearly as old as

Rocket and just as feeble. "As good as it gets at this point. Like my Rocket, we have to figure we're on borrowed time."

The minister's face shadowed, but Craig knew it did little good to foster false hope. Nothing lived forever. Tip and Rocket would be lucky to see another Christmas. North Country winters were hard on old pets.

"Well, then." The minister mustered his smile, but the effort cost him. "We'll enjoy the time we have, hmm?"

Craig gripped the older man's hand in a clasp of understanding. "Yes, sir."

Outside, the bright June day called to him. Seeing Sarah and the kids making their way to the pickup, he headed in their direction. "Sarah?"

She turned. For just a second he witnessed a glimmer in her eye. Expectation. Hope.

His heart tightened.

She glanced down. When she raised her gaze, her face was calm, those doe eyes quiet. "Yes?"

He wasn't going to let her get away that easy. "I haven't been properly introduced to your young friends."

"Tom's children."

She said it deliberately, studying his reaction. He swallowed the negative surge that dovetailed with Tom's name and smiled. Eyeing the tallest one, he stuck out his hand. "Olivia, right?"

She flushed with either pleasure that he knew her name or embarrassment over their initial roadside meeting. He smiled, trying to forget she was Tom's daughter. "Are you still running? I don't see you out on the roads."

She shrugged, awkward. A tiny smile softened her features. "Sometimes."

Craig nodded encouragement. "You've got talent. I saw you race when you were this high." His hand gesture indicated a smaller girl. "I expect that extra foot of height might be to your advantage."

Again she flushed. This time she dimpled. "Thank you."

"I'm Craig Macklin." Because Sarah seemed tongue-tied,

he made the introductions. "I'm building the house across the street from your Aunt Sarah's place."

"That's a nice house." Brett's note of appreciation was genuine. He reached out a hand. "I'm Brett."

"Oh, I remember you." Craig's reminder brought color to Brett's cheeks, but Craig laughed it off. "And that house has been a dream of mine for a long time. I'm glad you like it. And this is Aleta, right?" Eyeing the little girl, he cocked a look of interest to Sarah. "We met at Doyletown Day, remember?"

"Everybody calls me Skeeter," the little girl told him, her scrubbed-clean face surrounded by shiny, wavy curls. Quite a difference from the first time he saw her.

Craig appeared to weigh the information, then leaned in. "What do you like better? Aleta or Skeeter?"

"I like apple pancakes," she announced. "And these shoes hurt."

"Skeeter." Olivia sent her an impatient look. "Stop complaining. Seriously."

Craig stooped lower. "Mine do, too," he consoled her. "I think we should head home, put on comfortable shoes and have apple pancakes. What do you say?"

"Are you coming to our house?" Skeeter smiled, Shirley Temple dimples peeking from opposite sides of the grin.

"Well…" He sent an expectant look to Sarah, then shrugged. "I don't know."

She looked flummoxed and none too happy, but nodded. "You're more than welcome, Dr. Macklin."

He opened the truck door and hoisted Skeeter into the middle of the extended cab's back seat. "Craig, please, Sarah." He looked down, meeting Sarah's gaze, letting his eyes twinkle into hers. "We are neighbors."

The emphasis on her name brought color to her cheeks. "Yes."

"Then I think first names are in order." He didn't give her an out, just followed her to the driver's door and opened it for her. She started to say something, but reconsidered. Lips tight, she gripped the wheel to pull herself up.

Craig guided her movements, then stepped back, ignoring her look of chagrin. "Half an hour, give or take?"

She looked trapped, but nodded.

"Good. See you then." Craig stepped back to allow her space to pull away. He weighed things up as her tailgate diminished in size.

She didn't look back. Bad sign. But then, he had no clue why he'd cornered her in the first place. What was he thinking?

Just being neighborly, he assured himself as he strode to his SUV. *I'm following my mother's words of wisdom. To have good neighbors, be a good neighbor.* Extending good will was in everyone's best interests.

Sarah didn't always come to Holy Trinity. He knew she sometimes took the kids to their church in Potsdam. Of late, he'd seen her here every time he'd come. Frowning, he fought the nudge of guilt about the Sundays he'd missed.

Her presence used to bother him. Old anger enveloped him, even in church, hardening him when he should have been praying for compassion and understanding. No amount of prayer could reclaim what his grandparents had lost. The worry and suffering they'd endured. Craig had resented that. In turn, he'd resented Slocums in general. Sarah's simple presence had been a reminder, a thorn in his side.

He hadn't bothered praying about it. Inclusive anger felt justified after Tom's actions.

Reading Sarah's eyes changed his perceptions, pushing him to see Sarah, the woman. Faithful. Kind. Stalwart. Ambitious.

Studying the two-lane road, Craig recognized the depth of his sin. He'd lumped them together, a single entity, and that was wrong.

He slid into the driver's seat. A small part of him felt sorry for Sarah's current circumstance, although she wasn't the type to encourage pity. No, Sarah's panache inspired…admiration. She was small, but tough. A doer, not unlike his mother.

Brooks would have referred to her as hardwood, all the

way. Strong but pliable. Not a hint of veneer. Craig scrubbed his hand across his face as realization seeped in.

What was he thinking?

Something about Sarah tugged his consciousness. Maybe it was her singularity, a need for a friend. Someone who didn't mind grimy clothes and smudged boots, all part of a day's work in farm country.

Wanting something to give her, Craig stopped at McMorency's farm and bought a half-gallon jug of maple syrup and two quarts of fresh berries, definitely a more country boy token of appreciation.

Grinning, he climbed into the front seat and headed to Pierrepont.

Sarah viewed the house with dismay. Not as bad as Rita's, but nothing to entertain in, either. Why had she said yes? Let herself get trapped into serving Craig Macklin food? What was wrong with her?

She'd tended the sheep early, intending to straighten up the house after church. The clock said nearly noon and Craig was due any minute. Nothing was tidy, despite the ten minutes of effort the kids put in.

A light knock sounded. Drawing a frazzled breath, Sarah moved to it, unsure what to say or do. Six feet plus of good-looking man stood there, holding a jug. As he stepped in, he handed the bottle to her. She eyed the container, turning her hand. "What is this?"

His look said that should be self-explanatory. Her cheeks warmed as she corrected her question. "Why did you bring this?"

"To be nice."

Unmoving, unexpressive, she met his gaze. She wanted him uncomfortable, to remember the times he hadn't been nice. The times he'd looked through her, as though she didn't exist. The occasions when he'd ignored her in a group or a crowd, disavowing her presence. He took the look solidly, then broke it by quoting, "Tend my sheep. Feed my lambs."

His reminder of the morning's gospel brought more heat to her face. Obviously he'd been listening. He smiled at her reaction while he eyed the kitchen. "How old is this place?"

She read censure in the question. "Old."

"Old doesn't equate with bad." His tone was mild. Not aggressive.

"It needs work," she admitted, not meeting his gaze. She didn't want him noting the dusty shelves, the clutter on her desk, the rugs that needed vacuuming. All things she'd do if there were more hours in the day.

But she wasn't about to make excuses. She hadn't expected company, and he could either like it or lump it. He moved forward and studied the spinning wheel alongside the wood stove, then fingered the colorful skeins hanging above. "You spin?"

"Not now."

"Not now," he repeated, thoughtful. His fingers grazed the wheel's pale finish. Fingers that looked strong and hearty, but gentle, too. "Because…?"

Sarah busied herself at the counter. "No time. I learned in college. The woman who owned the farm I worked on had a wheel. She showed me. In New Zealand I had lots of time to practice. Nights are long there. Now…" she hesitated and turned, her eyes on the treadle machine. "It's on hold for awhile. My sheep don't produce the kind of wool a hand-spinner would choose, anyway."

"Too coarse."

"Yes." She looked up, surprised he knew the difference. He wasn't exactly sheep-savvy like Hank. "I could buy fleeces and card them, but right now my time should be used for other things." Swallowing a sigh she stepped forward and smoothed her hand across the golden wood. "Someday."

Liv appeared, with Brett on her heels. "The bathroom's not disgusting any more," she sang out. "Hi, Dr. Macklin."

He grinned at Sarah's discomfiture, then turned his attention to the kids, noting their jeans. "More comfortable?"

"Yeah. Wanna see the pups?"

He looked torn, his eyes going from Sarah to the adolescents. "Is there time?"

Sarah nodded to the big bowl. "The batter's ready. They won't take long to cook. Five minutes?"

"All right." He nodded to Liv and Brett. "Lead the way."

The smell of apples and cinnamon filled the house as Craig and the kids walked back in. Sarah raised a brow as each child set a quart of berries on the counter. "Beautiful berries. Where…?"

Craig jumped in. "I grabbed them at McMorency's when I got the syrup. I couldn't carry them in without crushing the berries, so Brett and Liv helped."

"They're great." Liv chewed as she spoke, bobbing her head in appreciation. "I love fresh berries."

"Me too," chimed Brett.

Craig moved closer to Sarah. "And you, Miss Slocum? How do you feel about fresh berries?"

Right now she felt as silly as she'd ever felt in her life. "They're…nice." She lifted her shoulders in a little shrug.

"Nice?" He took another step forward. There was no missing the breadth of him. The warmth. His short-sleeved shirt showcased arms toned by work, the muscles sharply defined. She gulped and nodded.

"Very nice."

"Ah." He grinned.

Unintentionally, she met his smile with one of her own.

Drat. Double drat. Where were her Abenaki skills when she most needed them? The ability to meet any situation in full control, shadowing her feelings.

The practiced reserve had served her well for years. She'd unnerved Tom and Ed no small number of times, employing that impassive stare. Much more effective than lashing out, which would give her half brothers satisfaction and control. Just what they wanted.

They didn't get that from her. She was strong. One with the

Spirit, unafraid to turn a blank face and deaf ear to negatives around her.

But her well-honed methods didn't seem to work on positives. Craig's smile made her want to answer it in kind. His gentleness inspired hers.

Dangerous, to open her heart like that, especially to someone who equated her with bottom feeders not too long ago. But then, she hadn't thought too highly of him, either.

By the time they'd consumed fruit-studded pancakes, an easy calm pervaded. Skeet was sated and therefore happy, at least momentarily. Liv rinsed plates and Brett loaded the sink with wash water.

"No dishwasher?"

Craig stood at the door, ready to leave. He nodded to the sink full of bubbles.

"I don't usually need one," Sarah explained. "Now I've got two." Her look swept Brett and Livvie.

Liv groaned.

Brett made a face, then asked, "Can we head to Mom's when we get done? I've got to grab a few things."

"Yes. I'll walk Dr. Macklin to his car—"

"Craig," he corrected for at least the third time. She ignored him.

"—then I'll be back."

He swung open the wooden screen door, holding it wide as she stepped out. The higher angle of the sun brought long-awaited warmth until they stepped beneath the trees. There it was cool. Sarah resisted the shiver, stoic to the end.

"Thank you for breakfast." Craig hesitated, then bent closer as Sarah maintained her silence. "I shouldn't have railroaded you like that."

"It was fine." She didn't meet his look.

"It wasn't." He paused, studying her, picking his words. In a gentle gesture he grasped her upper arm. The warmth of his touch soothed the chill of the shade. "I forgot all you have to do. The work here." He nodded to the barn and the fields. "The accounts. The kids. When Liv talked about how you helped with her final homework project, I realized it embarrassed you that your house wasn't ready for company."

She bit her lip, looking at anything but him.

"I made it awkward for you. I'm sorry."

Sarah lifted a shoulder.

"The pancakes were great."

She glanced up. Hints of green and gold danced in his eyes. Eyes that matched the sandy-brown tones of his hair, short as it was. Eyes that scanned her face, her gaze, then came to rest on her mouth, his look warm. Inviting.

She stepped back. "I have to go."

He nodded and squeezed her arm. She tried to pretend his touch meant nothing. Did nothing. Surely he wouldn't notice her flush?

"Thanks again."

She kept her reply short, hoping he wouldn't note the tremor in her voice. "You're welcome."

"Not 'come again'?"

He was teasing. She knew it from the sound of his tone, the look in his eye, but she'd never played this game and he'd played it way too often if rumors ran true. The heat infusion deepened. She nearly stuttered. "Thanks for the syrup. The berries, too."

Craig's eyes crinkled. He angled his head. He looked nice. Approachable. Friendly.

Too friendly.

Strong, broad fingers tightened against the soft skin of her upper arm, his touch doing strange things to her heart, her belly. He flashed her one last, gentle smile before releasing her arm. "You're welcome, Sarah."

Chapter Ten

Startled awake, Craig eyed his cell phone. Did it ring? An emergency call?

No way. Not on his weekend off. He squinted through sleep-deprived eyes. The digital display flashed twelve fifty-two. Then fifty-three. He stretched back out, plumped his pillow, closed his eyes and decided he must have been dreaming.

Woof. Woof. Woof.

The baritone bay dragged Craig's eyes open once more. Ah, yes. That was in the dream. A dog calling him.

Woof.

Rubbing his eyes, Craig peered at the clock a second time.

Twelve fifty-five.

Woof... Woof... Woof, woof, woof...

Somebody's dog wasn't happy. The only one close enough to have a dog he would hear was Sarah.

Stretching, Craig grumbled. The big white dog was barking a warning. Another dog, maybe? Coyote? There'd even been unsubstantiated reports of wolves moving into the area although the DEC wouldn't admit it.

As a shepherd, Sarah must be used to these wake-up calls. No doubt she'd handle it. Turning a deaf ear to the deep-toned chorus, he laid back down, attempting to sleep.

By one-ten he realized the error in his assumption. The first Maremma's warning had been joined by another's.

Great. Harmony.

Shrugging into warm clothes, Craig laced his boots with tired hands. Being dragged out of bed wasn't unusual for a country vet. Resenting it like crazy on his first weekend off in three weeks seemed understandable. Resigned, he pushed open the door of the camper and trotted down the drive.

Minutes later he zeroed in on the problem.

Sheep wandered, unfenced. Picking his way along the front edge of the field, he blessed the nearly full moon, but wished for more warmth. Glad he'd grabbed his work gloves, he shoved his hands into them, glaring at the steam his breath produced in the chill, north air.

A deep-throated growl sounded nearby.

Craig hesitated.

A broad, white, teeth-baring dog, hackles raised, planted himself in front of the tired vet.

Hesitation became a dead stop.

Picking out the pale canine among the white sheep was a trick in broad daylight. A good guard dog maintained a low profile, blending with its charges until needed.

Obviously the dog felt needed now. Another low growl convinced Craig to stay still, acclimate the dogs to his presence.

Or run as fast as he could.

He tossed that idea and perched on the nearest stump. The sheep wandered at will. He had no clue where they belonged, or how to get them back there, but he couldn't walk away and leave them untended. Even stupid creatures like sheep deserved a chance in the dead of night.

He turned and surveyed Sarah's yard. Mercury vapor lights brightened the barnyard, but no additional lights glimmered from the house. Working his jaw, he decided to wait. Whatever had pushed the flock through the tensile fencing could be lingering on the perimeter.

That idea had him finding a more comfortable position. He wished he'd grabbed a zip-top bag of his mother's venison jerky. His father always said the woman was part squaw when it came to preparing game meat.

The thought put him in mind of the sleeping shepherdess. Squaw.

What kind of term was that considered now? Factual? Derogatory? He'd Google it, check the origin. It wouldn't do to insult a young woman who was obviously a lot better at ignoring late-night canine danger calls than her neighbor seemed to be.

Sarah tumbled into bed, dead on her feet. The new round of lambs was dropping with few casualties, but the influx of homework, exam preparation and nighttime accounting made for short sleep.

Real short.

Her head ached and her brain disengaged at will. Crawling into bed at midnight, she was awakened sometime later by the deep baying of a Maremma. Then another.

Trouble. She peered at the clock, blinked, rubbed her eyes and peered again. Two-fourteen.

She fought an emotional overload brought on by stress and lack of sleep. Tugging on layers to ward off the spring chill, she stuffed gloves into her pocket and grabbed her shotgun, just in case.

Chapter Eleven

"Please don't shoot me."

Sarah froze, fingers tight against the smooth stock.

"It's Craig, Sarah. Put down the gun." The calm in his voice sounded forced.

"What are you doing here?"

Smooth, Sarah. What do you think the guy's doing here with a chorus of barking dogs in the middle of the night?

Considering her recent schedule, she decided to cut herself some slack.

"One of us can't sleep through the incessant barking of big white guard dogs," Craig explained.

Sarah drew a breath of consternation, then slipped the shotgun behind the seat. "They woke you?"

Wasn't this exactly what she feared? That the dogs or sheep would bother him? Annoy him?

In turn, he would annoy her. Wonderful.

Craig pretended a glance at a nonexistent watch. "About two hours ago."

"I'm so sorry." Frowning, she narrowed her eyes in frustration. "I didn't hear them."

Craig's look swept from the field to the house and back, clearly indicating the abbreviated distance. "Can I borrow a set of those earplugs?"

Sarah dropped her gaze. "I always hear them," she muttered, thinking out loud. "How could I...?"

"Tired?"

His gentle note of concern sent a flutter within. Fierce, she shut it down. "That's no excuse."

He changed the subject. "I wasn't sure how to re-pen them and I didn't want to make the situation worse, so I just sat here. That calmed the Maremmas for a while, until someone's Lab mix rooted around the outside of the upper pen. They started up again as if they expected me to do something."

"A Lab?" Sarah drew her brows together. "Black?"

"Black and tan." Craig straightened. "It was pretty dark."

"I don't know of any dogs like that in the area," Sarah mused. She gave a sharp whistle that brought a Border collie running. "You're solo, Max. Away." Nodding, she motioned right and gave a short, low whistle. The dog raced off, rounding sheep in counterclockwise fashion. Sarah moved ahead, skirting the grassy edge, angling toward the lower left corner of the upper pasture. She gave another whistle, higher this time. "Come bye, Max."

Pivoting, the dog herded the western edge, working the group in quick, steady fashion. She saw Craig study the dog's self-corrective techniques and angled her head toward the obedient flock. "He's made for this. An instinctive herder. I hardly had to train him."

"The best trainers think the dog trains himself."

Sarah flushed at the compliment. Grateful for the diminished moonlight, she fought the flurry of feelings his words brought.

He was being nice again, completely out of character.

And disconcerting.

And incredibly pleasant.

Most likely because of their new proximity. He was about to be her closest neighbor. Obviously he thought sharing a peace pipe a better way to start that relationship than hauling the sheriff out of his office in the middle of the night to complain about her noisy dogs. Speaking of which...

"This happens sometimes," she explained. "The Maremmas take their guarding tasks seriously." She let her eyes glance into his. He nodded.

"Figured that part out when they bared their teeth at me."

Again his voice was nonchalant. Steady and even. Sarah gulped. "Did they really?"

Craig shrugged, his attention tuned to the maneuvers of the black and white spitfire channeling sheep through the fence gap. Moving left, Sarah maneuvered post and wire into a quick semblance of order.

"Isn't that hot?" Craig moved up behind her, his voice concerned, eyeing the electric fence.

"I unplugged it before I got in the pickup. Just in case it was tangled."

Silence ensued while she reconfigured the wire and post to her satisfaction. Craig broke the quiet by noting, "They're in."

"Max." The single word brought the small collie to her side, and then he trotted toward the barn, head high.

"Nice." Appreciation marked Craig's voice.

Fighting a smile, Sarah slipped the next post into alignment, then untwisted the wires with a flip of her wrists. "A good dog."

Again the silence stretched. Craig studied her movements. Once done, she stepped back and blew on her chilled fingers. "It's June. The thermometer could start to climb anytime now."

"We say that every June," Craig agreed, falling into step as she walked the south end. All appeared well, the wire tense and unyielding. He nodded to the disappearing collie. "Rocket used to run like that."

She glanced up, puzzled.

"My dog."

"Oh."

"A chocolate Lab," he continued, his voice warm. "The kind of dog a kid could grow up with." He pushed his hands into the front pocket of his sweatshirt. "He's old now. I've had him since high school."

"'Tis pity not to have a dog, whatever be his breed," Sarah quoted Edgar Guest. "For dogs possess a faithfulness, which humans sadly need."

"Exactly," Craig agreed. "Rocket's pretty accepting."

"How old is he?" Scanning the fence one last time, Sarah turned toward the work-worn pickup.

"Nearly fifteen."

Sarah knew what that meant. She paused her step. "I'm sorry."

Craig jerked a shoulder. "What happens, happens."

His tone belied the words. Sarah almost winced. "Of course." Nodding to the truck, she waved a hand to the passenger side. "I'll drive you home."

"No need." Craig paused, watching her. She almost flinched under his scrutiny. His next words tightened her jaw. "Get some sleep, Sarah. You look like you could use it."

He may have meant it kindly, but she heard chastisement. He thought she looked tired. Haggard. Her mind leapt to the negatives her half brothers heaped on her over the years. The reproaches and jeers. Snide remarks that made a young girl question her worth and her beauty.

She fought a retort, struggling to separate the present from the past. When she was tired, it was hard to do. Nodding, she climbed into the truck, cranked it around and was back in bed before Craig Macklin's feet started the ascent of his driveway.

Served him right.

Chapter Twelve

How could you do that? How could you do that? How could...
Sarah's thoughts ran through her mind like a freight train the next morning.

Craig had been nice to her. Kind enough to play Little Boy Blue to her Sleeping Beauty before she drove off in a huff because he noticed she looked tired.

She was tired. It would take more than seven hours of segmented sleep to make up for a chain of abbreviated nights, but it would all turn out for the best. She had to believe that.

Didn't Job have his trials? And Moses, the recalcitrant leader, dealt with chronic doubt, confusion and insubordination from the people he led.

Given that, Sarah White Fawn Slocum should be able to handle multiple sheep herds, three rowdy children, two messy homes...

And a partridge in a pear tree...

Right.

She spied Livvie curled up with a book. "Cleaning today. Your house, this time."

Liv nodded, surprising Sarah. "I'm ready. Brett's feeding the barn sheep."

"Really?" Sarah angled her head. Took a moment. "Thanks for the coffee."

"No problem. I put the cleaning supplies we might need in the truck."

Sarah walked over and felt the girl's forehead. "Are you feverish? Tired?"

Livvie frowned. "No."

"Then who are you and what have you done with my niece? Are you a pod person?"

Liv burst out laughing, then sobered. "I just figured you must be tired to sleep until almost nine o'clock." She shrugged. "And I wanted to do something to help Mom."

Sarah hugged her. "Me, too. I want the house decent when she comes home. Give her a fresh start."

"It might take more than a day," warned Liv.

"But we can get a lot done. We'll make a list, check it twice."

"Find out who's naughty and nice?" Liv laughed. "A little out of season, Aunt Sarah."

And then some. Two Christmas references in a span of minutes. Must be the cold nights. "Gather up Skeets, will you? I'll help Brett so we can hit the road. I want to check Lili's pups, too. The ad goes out this week."

"I'll miss them."

Sarah lifted a wry brow. "Missing them would require stepping foot in the barn."

"That's true," Liv replied, fingering a strand of hair. "But as long as I walk straight to the pups, it isn't so bad."

Sarah leveled a look at the teen, then smiled. "Get your sister."

"It's worse than I remembered."

Liv's early optimism disappeared when a ripe smell assaulted their senses at Rita's door.

Brett looked around, overwhelmed.

Skeeter grabbed Sarah's hand. "What's wrong?"

Sarah moved forward, toting supplies. "Not a thing, honey."

Disillusionment marked the faces of the older two. Sarah jerked her head left. "Let's start with opening the windows.

Air things out. Brett, I'll have you clear out the living room. I've got a giant box of garbage bags here." Her nod indicated the bright yellow box. "Skeets, your job will be to find all the toys and put them in—" Sarah glanced around "—that box right there. We'll sort them later. Liv?" She eyed the girl at her side. "I'm going to start on the kitchen and back porch. You want to help me or tackle the upstairs?"

The look on Livvie's face could have gone either way. Explode or implode. Exhaling, she headed to the stairs. "I'll straighten up first. Then dust and vacuum. Scrub the bathrooms."

Sarah sent her a woman-to-woman smile, then eyed Skeeter. "Now, Skeets, the important thing is, don't get in Brett's way. He's got a big job ahead of him. Brett." She turned to the boy, who looked somewhat overcome. "Would you rather I help you in here? Give it a head start?"

He considered that for a moment, looking hopeful, then manned up. "Naw." He glanced at his little sister, unusually cooperative, and nodded. "We can handle it. Can you keep the door open, though?" His gaze slid to the swinging door separating the kitchen from the living room.

He didn't want to be alone with the mess. The smells.

"Absolutely. That way we can talk as we work. You guys want music?" Moving to the CD system, she raised a brow.

Skeets twirled. "Taylor Swift!"

Brett groaned, then grinned. "How about the theme from *Rocky*? We sure have a fight on our hands."

"*Rocky* first," Sarah decided, ignoring Skeets' groan. "Then Taylor. We might follow her up with a little Kenny Chesney, or maybe some Michael W. Smith." She eyed the room, then the boy. "I'll be in the kitchen. If anything tries to eat you, holler."

"Right." He scanned the room with an Oscar-worthy look. "If I live to tell about it."

The day flew. Sarah pulled out all the stops and did takeout for lunch, grateful for proximity to the golden arches, then ordered Chinese for dinner. By that time the living room invited repose, throw rugs were aired and thrashed, the kitchen sparkled with a new coat of lemon polish to the chestnut-toned cupboards, counters gleamed and the floors shone.

"The dining room looks good, Aunt Sarah." A warm smile softened Liv's features. "I forgot how pretty it was."

Sarah nodded. "Me, too. I love the bay window. It's a shame it overlooks the neighbor's driveway."

"You're used to acres of privacy. This is normal to us."

"Country mouse, city mouse?"

Liv's smile deepened. "I don't think I'd like being a real city mouse. New York or something like that. But being in town?" Her look encompassed the neighborhood. "I like being near people."

"I don't."

Sarah looked at Brett, noting the strength of the assertion. Her expression invited him to continue.

"I hate it."

"Why?" Keeping her voice level, she allowed Brett time. If he was offering the rarity of sharing his feelings, she'd give him whatever proved necessary.

"Everybody watches us. Waits for us to mess up."

"They do not." Liv jumped in, her tone absolute.

Brett went silent, rolling his eyes.

Sarah considered his allegation, thoughtful. "Some do," she acknowledged. "Your dad's actions made things difficult. It takes time for people to move beyond that. See you for who you are."

"Mom's drinking doesn't help," Liv noted.

"You're right. I think she got overwhelmed and didn't know where to turn. She felt let down by her husband. By God. Her family." Seeing their looks, she corrected herself. "Not you guys. Her extended family. Uncle Ed and Aunt Heather. Grandpa. They blamed her because they couldn't accept your father's guilt. It had to be someone else's fault and your mom was a handy target. It got to be too much."

"But she's a grown-up." Brett's tone said he thought that

made you invincible. How Sarah wished that was true. She made a quirky face.

"Yeah. But we grown-ups have our problems. Sometimes we get hung up on them. Forget to take them to God. It's easy to get in over our heads."

"Has that ever happened to you?" Liv's expression said she couldn't believe anything overwhelmed Aunt Sarah.

Sarah met the look. "Yes. That's part of the reason I went to New Zealand after college. Some people don't like the fact that I've got an interesting heritage on my mother's side."

"Because you're Native American?"

"Yes. And part African-American on my grandfather's side. Slocums don't handle diversity well. Once my mother died, I wasn't welcome at most family functions. I got tired of being left out."

"But…" Brett screwed up his face. "You always sent us presents. Birthday and Christmas stuff. And cool cards."

Sarah rumpled his hair. "Of course I did. I love you. We're family."

"Dad didn't like you," Liv remarked.

Sarah shrugged. "Your father liked control. I had a mind of my own."

"You were independent."

Inside, Sarah marveled at the girl's intuition. Outside, she kept her face placid. "I am. And I have a deep faith that frightens some."

"Because they don't believe?"

Sarah considered that. "Because I believe so fully. Faith is a gift. Not everyone accepts it."

"Grandpa likes me." Skeeter light-stepped her way into the kitchen, her left cheek covered in pink sleep wrinkles. She stretched and yawned. "He says I look like my daddy's mother."

Liv snorted. "You look like Mom did when she was little. We've got pictures that prove it."

"We do?" Skeeter's voice rang with doubt, making Sarah realize Skeets hadn't experienced normal things like viewing old pictures. She'd been a toddler when her father died. Since then…

"Let's finish eating, then we'll look at pictures. After that, back to work."

"Awwww…" Brett looked as dismayed as he sounded.

"Tough it out, kid. We've got a timeline." Sarah pointed to the wall calendar. "The Bristol boys are tending the flock today, but we have church in the morning right after farm chores."

Sarah ignored Liv's groan. "And your Mom is due home tomorrow afternoon. We want things shipshape, right?"

Their agreement was halfhearted this late in the day, but Sarah didn't care. She pushed back from the table. "Skeets, you hungry?"

Skeeter eyed the white containers, suspicious. "Do we have apple pancakes?"

"Not tonight. If you have some of this chicken or beef, I'll make you apple pancakes in the morning." *Mental note: set alarm early. Great.*

"I don't like this stuff. It's yucky."

"Then no apple pancakes tomorrow."

Brett gaped. Liv almost smiled. It had been a long time since Rita set boundaries for Skeeter. The little girl's lower lip popped out beneath a really exaggerated frown.

"But I don't like it."

Sarah kept her face noncommittal. "I heard you, sweetheart. You won't starve, I promise."

"We can always have oatmeal in the morning," Liv offered, driving home Sarah's point. "With walnuts."

Sarah fought a smile as she stood. "I'll leave the food out in case you change your mind."

"But—"

Brett headed upstairs to retrieve the pictures, then turned. "Can we finish up first, then do pictures? There's not that much left to do."

Sarah turned Liv's way. "What do you think?"

"Works for me."

"All right." Sarah headed to the kitchen for a basin. Liv took a bucket of suds to the front porch, her face determined.

As Sarah scrubbed the downstairs bathroom, she joined Kenny Chesney in a duet about how forever feels. Scrubbing cleanser across the sink's surface, the words brought to mind thoughts of commitment. Love. Marriage.

Craig Macklin's image appeared and refused to be shoved away. Scowling, she mounted a second attack on the shower stall, scrubbing to beat the band. When her mind refused to be cleared of jumbled pictures of Kenny and Craig, romance and Craig, forever and Craig, she marched to the living room, changed the CD, noted that Skeets was taking mini bites of sweet and sour chicken, then squared her shoulders as the background tones of Michael W. Smith lent a more spiritual air to the cleaning spree.

Right until he launched into his beautiful rendition of "Do You Dream of Me?"

She drew a breath. A really deep one, then gave the toilet the best scouring it had known in some time, working hard to erase thoughts of Craig Macklin's easy humor and strong hands from her mind.

Chapter Thirteen

"Come on, old man." Craig tried to coax Rocket from the backseat of the SUV, figuring a warm evening romp would do the old boy good.

Nope.

He held out a hand of appeal. "Let's take a walk. I'll show you around the place. Start getting you acclimated."

Rocket lay along the back seat, head tucked, obviously way too comfortable and tired for Craig to tempt him off the soft seat. Years back, Rocket would have leapt at the chance to get into a car, take a road trip. He bounded through fields, sniffing out this and that, studying terrain, ears cocked, chest out, legs braced, gaze locked. A hunter's stance.

No more. Despite Craig's best efforts and medical intervention, Rocket showed his age. Leaving him to nap on the plush seat, Craig headed down the drive, then walked the road's edge, drinking in the pastoral setting. Grazing sheep bordered his right, fresh hay lots lay to his left. The scent of sun-warmed country pervaded, the rustic situation balanced by songbirds garnering a last feeding.

Laughter drew his attention right. He saw nothing but grazing sheep, peaceful and calm. Jaws moved, rhythmic, underscoring the contentment of a well-kept flock. They made a pretty picture, their creamy forms a complement to the deciduous woods, making him wonder how something could be that nice-looking and yet so dim-witted. He knew from forensics class that sheep were actually born with a brain, but no amount of research proved they actually used it. Craig shook his head and walked until another aberrant sound interrupted the halcyon setting.

He turned, scanning the pasture with more diligence, tracking the noise.

A cackle rose from a grassy knoll, then a figure appeared, followed by another. The pitch of the field had hidden them until now. The child spun with glee, twisting and twirling in the summer sun.

The second figure did likewise, trim jeans suiting her petite frame, the coral knit top showcasing really nice curves, her tawny skin offsetting the color to perfection. He watched, drawn to the camaraderie, the shared joy of child and woman as they moved up the field. Their laughter, bright and free, provided a perfect balance to the placid sheep, the singing birds. It was a summer sound and he stood silent, appreciative.

"Craig!" Skeeter barreled his way, pigtails flying. Sarah followed in quieter fashion, a familiar rise of gold tingeing her color.

"The fence is hot," he warned as Skeeter drew close.

She nodded. "I won't touch it. Can you walk with us?"

His glance to Sarah noted her discomfort. All the more reason to agree, he supposed. "I'd love to, but you're in there and I'm out here."

"Can't you just walk right there?" Skeeter pointed to the grassland running above the drainage ditch. "Just don't fall in."

"I could," he answered, catching Sarah's eye. She glanced down, then away. "You girls sounded like you were having fun."

"Oh, we were," caroled Skeeter, laughing up at Sarah. "We're princesses who escaped from a fire-breathing dragon. Aaaaarrrrrrgggggghhhh." She emitted an impressive pseudo-reptilian noise.

"How did you get trapped by the dragon?" Craig asked, appraising Sarah. "I would think your aunt's defensive skills would render most dragons powerless."

Her chin rose. Her shoulders straightened. Her gaze remained steady. Definitely not as amused as he'd hoped.

"The wicked prince," explained Skeeter, oblivious to the adult interchange. "There were two brothers. One was very, very good." Her eyes widened in the telling, her voice serious. "He made sure everyone followed the rules and obeyed the law. He was kind and gentle. Everyone loved him."

Craig nodded. "Sounds like a good guy. What happened next?"

Skeeter shook her head, eyes wide and sad. "His evil brother built a house close to the princesses' castle."

"He did, huh?" Craig chanced a glance at Sarah. Eyes down, she studied something of great import on the ground.

"Yes." Skeeter bit her lip at the injustice of it all. "Then he took us prisoner when the good brother wasn't looking. It was very scary."

"I'm sure." Glancing Sarah's way again, Craig smiled when she lifted her gaze. Cocking his head, he moved closer to the electric fence. "Are these mythical brothers familiar, my lady?"

"The author claims this to be a work of fiction and any similarities to peoples living or dead is purely coincidental," Sarah replied, her tone careful.

Craig faced her. Saw her lips twitch. At that moment he wanted to inspire her smile. Hear the laughter she'd shared with the child short moments before. Drawing conclusion from what he'd seen so far, Sarah Slocum didn't laugh often enough.

"It is, I'm sure, a fictional tale." Noting Skeeter's confusion, Craig clarified, "That means it's pretend. Made up. Of course—" he encompassed Sarah with his look, then played along "—I don't know any brothers like that around here."

"Do you know a lot of brothers?" Skeeter asked.

"Oh, yes." He gave a wise nod. "I know old brothers, young brothers, ugly brothers…"

She giggled.

"And some handsome ones as well," he assured her, keeping his tone refined. "Maybe some who've made mistakes. Been somewhat stupid." He hesitated and brought his look to Sarah. "But not evil, surely."

They reached the gate. Craig watched as Sarah maneuvered the hooked handle to allow their exit, then affixed the closures to reconnect the circuit. Free of the fence, Skeeter launched herself at him. He swept her up and planted a kiss on her soft cheek. "You smell good."

"Aunt Sarah let me use her special lotion. We smell just the same," the child bragged.

Craig leaned forward until his face brushed Sarah's hair. He drew a long, slow breath. Stepping back, he smiled at her nonplussed expression. "You both smell wonderful."

"Thank you." The child dimpled and squirmed at the compliment. Sarah didn't, but she didn't look combative, either. An improvement, perhaps?

"It has a pretty name, too," Skeeter prattled on. "What was it, Aunt Sarah?" Turning, the child offered her question with no trace of guile.

Sarah blushed. He smiled to see it, watching deeper tones canvass her tawny cheeks once more. Her discomfort made her seem younger. Less secure. Watching her, he decided it wasn't a feeling she'd had much experience with. "Spill it, Sarah. What's it called?"

She bit her lip and glanced away, then drew an exasperated breath. Turning back, she met his gaze, reluctant. "Meadow Romance."

He grinned and softened his expression. "Really?" Surveying her, he stayed silent, allowing the seconds to mount. Her hands tugged the side seams of her jeans as he bent, inhaling deeply. "Perfect."

"Well." She stepped back, clasping her hands. "I've got work."

He nodded, still holding Skeeter. "I'll walk you to the door."

"It's right there." Her look indicated the short distance between them and the house. Her tone said she wanted to be rid of him.

"We can't let it be said that the prince left the princesses unprotected with dragons about, can we?"

"Oh, no." Skeeter's pigtails danced. "The ground could be—" she paused, searching for words "—fraught with danger. Hidden traps, destined to foil the bravest knight."

"Arthurian?" He hiked a brow to Sarah, indicating he was pretty certain the first grader hadn't come up with that line on her own. "I would have expected Three Sisters. Brother Eagle."

"Legends and fairy tales cross cultural boundaries," Sarah informed him, her gaze flicking up to his. When it did, he felt a surge of warmth. Delicious. Delightful. Wonderfully surprising.

"Tell me more."

She made it up the first step, putting her almost at eye level. Looking startled by his sudden proximity, she advanced another stair, lengthening the distance. "I have to go."

"Of course." Still smiling, he set Skeeter down. "Thanks for walking with me, girls."

"We didn't," Sarah protested, her brow knit. "We—"

"Yes?" He angled his head, holding her gaze, keeping his look aimed at her.

She was bothered, that was plain enough. Frustrated, maybe? Aggravated, annoyed, perturbed? Absolutely.

Interested?

A good possibility. But wishing she weren't. Stepping back, he knew he'd hit the nail on the head but hadn't a clue what to do about it. Slocums and Macklins were fire and water, oil and vinegar. Not a good mix.

And try as he might, Craig couldn't move beyond his behind-the-scenes actions in the whole mess. How he'd encouraged Gramps to go big or stay at home. Brave words from a brash young man with little to lose.

He sighed inwardly, wishing he could go back. Change

things. Knowing he couldn't and that his actions had helped spur a chain of events that left his grandfather dead and his grandmother dependent.

But the depths of Sarah's deep brown eyes drew him. The intelligence and character intrinsic to this woman. Why on earth did she have to be a Slocum?

He doffed a nonexistent cap. "Ladies. My pleasure."

"Thanks, Craig." Skeeter giggled, pressing two dimpled hands to her mouth. "It was nice of you to rescue us."

"Oh, I think Princess Sarah had things well under control," he confessed, smiling. "You'd already escaped the cruel tyranny of the evil brother, remember. I just offered my cloak of protection for the end of your journey."

Another giggle. "You talk funny."

"Thank you." He raised his gaze to Sarah, now on the top step, one hand on the door. "A fine, good night to you, Princess Sarah."

She graced him with a regal tilt to her chin. Turning, she stepped inside. "And you, Sir Macklin."

Chapter Fourteen

"**H**ey."

Surprised, Craig looked up from the hook he'd just baited. "Hey, yourself. How's it going, Brett?"

The youth lingered on the upper edge of the slope leading to the Higley Water Flow. A bike bearing scars of love lay tipped along the bank. Craig nodded to the water as he cast. "You fish?"

The boy shrugged.

"Ever try it?"

Again the shoulders lifted. Craig thought back to their pancake conversation. From the look on the boy's face, Craig figured Livvie must be on his case again. Noting a slight dance of the bobber, Craig jerked the line and twisted the reel.

The pole bent, its arc testifying the fish's presence.

"You got one?"

"A nice one." Grinning, Craig pulled up the yellow perch, pausing the swing of the line with one hand. "Some good eating here."

"You eat them?" Brett eyed Craig, curious. "How?"

"Clean 'em. Fillet 'em. Fry 'em."

"You cut out their guts?" That picture hiked the boy's interest.

"All of them." Craig stressed the qualifier while keeping his eye on the fish. He nodded to a stringer in the water. "There's more."

The boy gaped. "Wow."

"Want to give it a try?"

Brett's masked look disappeared. "Can I? Really?"

"Sure." Craig pulled a worm from the bait bucket and worked to forget this was Tom's son. The kid's resemblance to his mother made it easier. "First, bait the hook. Like this." He showed Brett the technique, then handed him the worm. "Go for it."

Lips compressed, Brett finagled the writhing night crawler onto the barbed hook. It took a few attempts, and a grimace with the initial piercing, but he soon held it up for Craig's inspection. "Got it."

"Now, we cast it."

"I've seen that on TV."

"Great. This is a lightweight pole so you need to hang on to the rod when you snap your wrist. Don't throw the pole into the water. Like this." Illustrating the technique, he showed Brett the quick movement as the line flung free. The sound of the casting reel made a quiet tick, tick, tick in the air.

Brett watched, studying the look of the pole, the arc of the line. Craig reeled it in, then handed it off. "You try it."

The first cast bounced off the ground. The second flung the line onto the grassy embankment. The third dropped the line into the water directly below them. Craig nudged the boy's shoulder. "Getting closer."

Brett laughed, then scowled. "I'll get it."

"Sure you will. It's early, yet."

The line made a more accurate curve next time, landing near the deep water. Craig nodded approval before advising, "Watch your bobber. This has been a hot spot all afternoon. They like this corner in June. Come warmer weather, they move closer to the middle. Then I have to drop the boat in. Row out."

"Cool."

The bobber dipped. Brett leaned forward, studying the red and white sphere. "I think—"

"Yup. Your line locked?" Craig's look went to the reel.

"Yes, sir."

"Give it a clean jerk."

Brett did, but the line slackened. Craig shrugged. "Happens all the time. Sometimes you hook 'em. Sometimes you don't. Bring it in. Cast it out."

The nearly empty hook surprised Brett. "He ate my worm."

"That's a good sign. Means they're hungry. Bait it again, Brett. I expect he and his friends are still partying."

"You don't mind?" The boy looked up as though realizing his participation might impinge on Craig's afternoon. Craig shook his head.

"Not at all. It's good to have company." Saying the words, he realized it was true.

The boy's face went reflective, then cleared. "Me, too."

Craig read between the lines. *Male company.* Brett had been surrounded by women for years. That was okay, but with his mother's problems, it probably wasn't the best situation for an adolescent boy whose family ran scarce on good male role models.

Not too many weeks back, Craig would have laughed at the idea of nurturing the boy. The notion of befriending Tom Slocum's kid would have seemed absurd.

Not anymore. Brett's companionship revived a host of boyhood memories. Craig raised an eyebrow to the boy. "You run like Livvie does, Brett?"

Brett shook his head. "Naw. Never liked it. I used to play soccer. I liked that a lot." His voice deepened. Craig read regret in the tone. He nodded as Brett threaded another worm on the hook.

"Nice job. Let's see if our friends' appetites have been appeased."

Brett's second cast was a clean sweep of the arm and flick

of the wrist. Craig complimented him. "Well done. Want a beer?"

Brett's mouth dropped open. His eyes went wide, then he chuckled when Craig handed him a cold can of birch beer from the six-pack cooler. Craig popped the top on his soft drink, took a long pull, then sighed his appreciation. "Man, I love this stuff. Birch beer. Root beer. Ever have 'em with vanilla ice cream?" Angling his head to the younger boy, he gave him a knowing look. "Best soda around."

"Aunt Sarah calls them floats." Brett found a comfortable spot on the grassy incline, sat and watched his line. "You make sodas with syrup and club soda and ice cream. She used to do that in college."

"Did she?" Pulling a grass stem free, Craig chewed it, picturing Sarah working a soda bar, her braid unmussed, her small, capable hands blending treats. He smiled. "Floats, huh?"

"Yeah. She buys us one at Sam's Club when we go. As long as we don't hassle her. They're huge."

"Like everything at Sam's," Craig noted. "Hey. Check that line."

"I see it." The timbre of the boy's voice rose and squeaked. Craig winced in remembrance. Puberty. Brett didn't appear to notice, intent on his pole.

He forgot to set the reel. Line poured out, sending everything slack. He muttered under his breath, frowned, then carefully wound the whole mess in and checked his hook. "Didn't get him."

Craig nodded. "No. Plenty of worm there for another try. Give it a go."

The first cast was clean but too short. Once again the boy reeled in, his face a study in patience. The next sweep launched a higher arc and a good drop.

"Nice. Does Aunt Sarah like root beer floats, too?"

"You like her."

Craig stopped chewing while he reconfigured this conversational twist. "Sure I do. She takes good care of her animals."

"Right." Brett started to add something else but his bobber jiggled, sending tiny concentric ripples in motion. "I think…"

"Clean jerk," Craig instructed, rising.

Brett snapped his arm, then started reeling. As the struggling fish cleared the water, the boy's excitement went to fever pitch. "He's bigger than yours."

Craig laughed. "You're right. Good job." He reached forward and stilled the fish, keeping sharp-edged fins tucked. As Craig released the hook, he nodded approval. "Biggest of the day."

"Seriously? Cool." Brett's rapt expression erased the earlier shadows. He watched as Craig strung the fish, then baited the hook once more. "Can I try again?"

"Go for it."

Not too long later the fish quit biting. Brett sent Craig a puzzled look. "What happened?"

Craig shrugged. "Maybe they're done feeding. Or they might have moved on. In any case—" he stood, unwrapping himself from the ground with a stretch and a yawn "—we can't eat them unless we go to step two. Want to learn how to clean fish?"

"With a knife?" Brett's eyes gleamed.

"A sharp one," cautioned Craig, tugging the stringer free. "We'll clean them at my place, then I can bury the remains."

"A fish funeral?" Brett looked puzzled.

Craig laughed and cuffed Brett's shoulder. "Yeah. A fish funeral. Call the choir." Seeing Brett's embarrassment, Craig nudged him again. "Fertilizer. We zip off the skin, cut out the part we eat, then bury the skeleton and the innards to enrich the soil. Nothing's wasted."

"Aunt Sarah says the soil around here is good," offered the boy as he walked alongside, carrying the pebbled-finish tackle box. "She says this is perfect sheep country."

"She should know. She's got a hand with them, that's for sure." Craig pictured her as he'd seen her in the moonlight, a small, dark form amongst the ghost-toned sheep. Small hands, strong and sturdy, fixing wire, straightening posts, not a hint of polish in sight. Her affinity with the dogs, so important to good shepherding.

"We're selling the Maremma pups."

Craig interpreted Brett's statement. "Rough, huh?"

"Yeah." Brett hunched his shoulders. "Molly's babies will be around awhile, but the big pups have to go."

"Many takers?"

"Aunt Sarah won't sell them to just anybody." Brett explained. "Some people wanted to buy one for a pet and she said no. Eight hundred dollars they were going to pay her." Brett ended the sentence with another squeak. Craig raised a brow of interest. "For a dog." The upswing of Brett's tone reflected his surprise. "And she said no."

Indignation mixed with surprise. Brett didn't want the pups to go, but couldn't understand refusing such a vast sum of money. Craig chose his words with care. "Sarah knows the dogs. Knows the breed. A Maremma without a job can get into trouble. They're bred to protect. Without a flock they can get too aggressive."

"That's what she said."

"So?"

They neared the SUV. Craig hit the remote to open the door. Together they stowed the fishing gear. Brett's face turned pensive. "Eight hundred dollars is a lot of money."

"It is." Craig stowed Brett's bike, then closed up the back before they climbed in. "But is it worth compromising your principles? Selling an animal into a situation that isn't right when you know it might cause problems later?"

"I guess not." Intent, the boy studied the road.

"Money's tight, huh?"

Brett's glance underscored his answer. "Yeah."

"It'll improve. My grandma says the tight times make the good times that much better." Grams had no idea how prophetic her words would be. And after decades of belt tightening, the sweet old gal ought to be able to relax without worrying where her next meal was coming from.

Oh, she knew her family would look after her. That wasn't an issue. But lack of independence for a stalwart old woman who'd earned every dollar she ever had? That was the problem. Not that she complained. Not her. No way, no how.

A sudden thought struck Craig as they pulled away. "You should call the house. Tell them you're with me and we've got some fish to clean. See if it's all right." From the look on the boy's face, Craig knew Sarah probably had no clue where he'd gone off to.

Brett hit the numbers with practiced ease. "Aunt Sarah? It's Brett. Yeah. I know."

Craig did his best to appear disinterested.

"I'm with Craig. We went fishing. He's going to teach me how to clean the fish now. If that's all right," he added, clutching the phone. Then, his voice tightening, he asked, "Did those people come? They took two?" His voice squeaked up again in surprise. "Did you give them a discount? Wow." He nodded, forgetting she couldn't see him. "Yeah, I'll come across once we're done over here." He said it as Craig's SUV made the climb to the new homestead. "'Bye."

"She sold two dogs?" Craig angled his head, regarding the boy.

"Yeah."

"Discount?"

"No way. She sold the girl for nine hundred so they gave her seventeen hundred all together."

"She's rich." In a grown-up world, Craig knew how quickly money disappeared. But the boy's mix of excitement at the money and displeasure at losing the dogs was palpable.

"She said we could get ice cream tonight to celebrate. And not just a cone, either. Whatever we want. A sundae, banana split…"

"Root beer float." Craig smiled at him. "Haul that stuff out of there, buddy, and let's get to work. Then I've got to grab a shower when we're done. I'm pretty fishy."

"You can come with us." Brett's invitation was sincere. Heartfelt.

His words made Craig hesitate.

He could go. It would be fun to head into town, buy an ice cream and share an evening with the kids. But what message would that send? People would be out in typical Sunday night fashion—couples strolling, kids skating. The custard stand stood in the middle of town, a popular meeting spot during the short months of summer.

Sarah had brushed him off pretty thoroughly. Not that he was a sensitive type of guy. His mother would roll her eyes at the very notion, then recount every clueless thing he'd done to prove her point.

But a man had to have standards. Principles. Something to stand firm on. When a woman waves you aside, a smart guy turns and runs, right?

Or stands his ground, making her see him. Notice him.

But the pressure of being seen together on "couples night" went too far. A Macklin keeping company with a Slocum? Oh, yeah, that would feed the North Country gossip mills. Fodder for a month, minimum. Then they'd watch for sightings of the two of them together, affirming the suspicion.

No. At this point he was fairly certain Sarah wouldn't welcome loose talk any more than he would. With Rita's problems, three kids to care for and two encompassing jobs, the woman was run ragged. It showed in her face, the shadowed circles beneath her pretty eyes.

More than pretty, actually. Deep. Dark. Warm eyes that said more than words ever could. He had a sudden memory of Sarah cradling Gino as he removed the invasive porcupine quills, her face nuzzling the dog's ruff, her voice crooning senseless words of love. Remembering, he wondered what it would be like to have her say those things to him? Hold him? Nuzzle his neck, her arms drawing him close?

He drew a really deep breath, shutting down his thoughts. Dangerous territory. Volatile. Explosive. Where had that come from?

He knew. He might not like it much, but he knew. Something in the young woman called to him. Sought him. In return, he longed to offer her shelter and warmth. His arms. His protection. His allegiance.

But it would never do. Craig couldn't stir up the hornets' nest by seeing Sarah Slocum.

Could he?

He motioned to Brett. "Can't do it tonight. Gotta work on the house." That, at least, was true. He angled his head to the crate Brett held. "Bring the box over here. We'll clean these guys out back and talk guy talk. Burp whenever we want and not say excuse me. Manly stuff."

Brett laughed. "Forget about girls."

"Exactly." With an almost physical nudge, Craig pushed thoughts of Sarah and ice cream firmly out of mind. Working on the house was definitely a safer alternative.

"I hear you're rich." Craig lounged in Sarah's barn door a couple of hours later, wondering what he was doing there. Hadn't he just waged a mental battle about this very thing?

Oops.

He grasped one side of the blocking board and helped slide it into place, then leaned in, admiring the five remaining Maremma pups. "Brett thinks seventeen hundred is a king's ransom."

Sarah's eyes softened in understanding. "At twelve, it is."

Craig nodded, his gaze on the little dogs. Two wrestled in the corner, evenly matched. Puppy growls and yips crescendoed and ebbed as first one, then the other gained advantage. Sarah shook her head. "Boys."

"Oh, yeah." Craig's smile went to a grin. "My mother has stories." He held out a plastic bag. "I brought some fish. Figured you could fry them for supper. If you've already eaten tonight, they'll be fine on ice until tomorrow."

"I—" She took the bag, her gaze turned out. After long seconds she looked back, then swallowed hard. "Thank you."

Those eyes. His throat thickened before he brought to mind his earlier list of objections. With effort, he broke the connection. "You're welcome. Brett found me at the Flow. We sat.

Did some guy stuff. I hope that's all right. I was wondering if he could work with me now and again. Interior stuff on the house. Maybe some yard work. With your permission."

She moved to the far end of the barn, weighing his offer, then pursed her lips. "Brett needs a man around. One he can look up to."

"Yes."

"But…" she paused, hesitant. It didn't take much for Craig to read her mind. Given his past behavior, allowing him extended time with an impressionable adolescent heightened her defenses. Narrowing his eyes, Craig followed her.

She advanced to the Border collie box. Murmuring words of affection she sat in the straw, lifting first one, then the other, talking to each baby dog.

Craig tried to stay aloof but a flop-eared female, blanketed in black, nuzzled his boots. Pretending resignation, Craig scooped the puppy up and talked to her. The pup preened, delighted. Craig eyed the little lady, then gave her Eskimo kisses.

"You're rubbing noses with a dog," Sarah pointed out.

"Best opportunity I'm anticipating for a while." Craig met her gaze and laughed.

Sarah looked dubious. "Strawberry-blond hair, flashy silver car, perfect nails and teeth, great shoes and short skirts. I don't think your prospects are as scarce as you make out."

"For a quiet woman, you take notice."

"The People have a saying," she replied, eyes down. "'One who talks a lot may hear nothing.' Quiet equates wisdom."

"I can't disagree." She squirmed under his gaze. Shifting his attention, he told the pup, "But I would think your Auntie Sarah might have noticed that the flashy silver car doesn't come around any more. Haven't seen the car or its owner in a long, long while."

She hesitated, her eyes on the pups. "It would be wrong to study my neighbor's home. Privacy is important."

Craig settled onto a nearby hay bale. "It is. But I've got a great view of your place from my front windows. The fields, the barn. Some of the house."

"Really?" She sounded annoyed. He hid the grin that inspired.

"Good views all around, actually." He set the pup in the straw, watching it work unsteady legs back to its mother. Unfolding himself from the hay bale, he stood. "Come see the house, Sarah. When you're not busy."

"I see from here." Calm and stoic, she stated the obvious.

"Not all of it." He let the pause grow, then added, "Walk over sometime. I'll give you a tour."

She didn't rise with him. Didn't agree. After long moments he started for the door.

"Craig."

She used his first name. Why did that make him feel so good? He turned. She brought her gaze to his. For just a moment her expression was young, trusting. Unguarded.

"Thank you for spending time with Brett. Offering him a job." She raised one shoulder, acquiescing. "I'm sure he'd love to help you. And it'll keep him out of Liv's way." She nodded to the plastic bag on the shelf. "I appreciate the fish. I'll tuck them into the fridge when I'm done with these guys."

He lifted the bag. "I'll do it. Then you don't have to hurry."

Mouth closed, she inhaled through her nose. Her chest rose and fell with the action, a soft cushion beneath the ribbed shirt, total woman. Her eyelashes fluttered. She nodded, then chewed the corner of her lower lip before pausing, regaining control. "Thank you."

Craig couldn't help himself. He reached down and smoothed a strand of thick, dark hair, allowing his hand to rest there, the feel of her hair, her skin, a summons. She stiffened, but he took his own sweet time to withdraw the hand, wondering what it would be like to kiss her. Hold her. Talk with her beneath the stars of things that had nothing to do with sheep. "Glad to do it."

He chastised himself all the way home. He should have sent

the fish with Brett. He'd spent the afternoon pushing thoughts of her away, unwilling to deal with the complexities of the situation. Forging a bond would arouse hurtful memories best left buried, and Rita had enough on her plate. That poor woman got way more than she bargained for in Tom Slocum, that's for sure. And after what he'd done to Grams, how could Craig rationalize dredging everything up by seeing Sarah?

Shouldn't, wouldn't, couldn't.

Despite all that, he'd walked the fish over himself. Petted her dog. Touched her hair.

That memory stopped him. Her hair, thick and heavy, bound and plaited but for one strand that escaped the braid. What would it be like to loosen that braid? Watch the dark waves tumble free?

He was treading dangerous ground and had no idea how to level the field. Maybe building here was a mistake. The proximity to Sarah made it difficult to keep thoughts of her at bay.

Or downright impossible.

What would You have me do, Father? What position am I in? On one hand is this woman who draws me like a moth to flame. It feels good to be drawn like that.

Craig worked his jaw, recalling his reactions.

Real good.

Why was he bothering God with this? Oh, he believed in the power of prayer. But God was too caught up with world affairs to straighten out the woes and worries of a North Country veterinarian attracted to the wrong girl.

And Rita? She'd been through enough. Her tenuous hold on sobriety shouldn't be challenged unnecessarily. And Craig didn't need constant reminders of his own foolishness, encouraging Gramps to invest.

The ramifications of his youthful shortsightedness had affected his entire family. Gramps was gone and Grams was living her older years shifting from house to house, a few months here, a few months there, an itinerant life when she should have been tucked safe and warm in a cozy home of her own.

Therein lay the answer. Not one he liked or welcomed, but a response nonetheless. Climbing the last yards to his half-finished home, he pushed thoughts of Sarah away.

But that hair…

Chapter Fifteen

Cream, brown and gold floral crepe swished past Sarah's hips, ending in a mid-calf swirl. Ivory heels gave her added height. Gold and cream earrings, fashioned from seeds and pearls, lent a Native American touch. She left her hair down, a choice she rarely made, letting the dark mass ripple across her back.

Plaited, her hair offered a definitive posture. Loose, it was open and free. Clipping the top with a bronzed barrette, she hoped Craig would be at church, then caught herself. Was it wrong to pray no one's animal got sick this particular Sunday, while she looked like something other than a farmer? She hoped not.

But why would she care if he was there or not?

Other than the obvious. Good-looking, funny, nice, caring and wore a great pair of jeans. Not to mention those roughed-up T-shirts.

The fact that he'd been less than friendly in the past should be a stern warning, although lately...

She shut down that train of thought as foolish and fairly stupid.

But that smile. Those eyes, amused and crinkled.

Enough, Sarah.

Rita opted not to go. Her first week home had been quiet

but constrained. Skeeter behaved naturally when her mother was around, but Brett and Liv walked on eggshells, too nice. Too compliant. "I'll catch the evening service," Rita explained, tension darkening her features. On the plus side, she was clean and unmuddled, her blond hair soft and lustrous once more. "There's a morning AA meeting in Potsdam. I want to talk with…"

"People who understand," finished Sarah.

"Yes. It's not that I don't appreciate your help," Rita continued.

Sarah cut her off. "Reet, we're fine. You know I'd do anything to help you. Maybe too much. It's okay to draw the line in the sand."

A ghost of a smile touched Rita's face. "Thank you, Sarah."

"Skeet, let's go. We'll be late." Eyeing her watch once Rita left, Sarah groaned. "Hustle up."

"I don't want to go." Rounding the corner, Skeeter clutched her midsection, distraught. "I don't feel good."

"A bellyache?" asked Sarah, concerned.

"She gets them whenever she doesn't want to go somewhere," accused Liv. "It gets her out of everything."

"Well, it's not getting her out of this," Sarah countered. "No apple pancakes for girls who skip church."

Skeeter's lower lip quivered but she squared her shoulders and scuffed her way to the truck.

Climbing in, Sarah asked, "We're set?"

Brett and Liv nodded. Skeeter moaned. Sarah noted the drama and chose to ignore it, hoping they wouldn't be late.

They made it just in time, slipping into a pew as the single bell tolled. She saw Craig to the left. He was two rows back, but she felt his presence as though he was next to her, sharing her songbook.

When they rose for the opening song, she felt Craig's gaze. A quick look confirmed the suspicion. He smiled, appreciation lighting his eyes.

But her choice of clothing had nothing to do with him, Sarah assured herself. Proper church attire set a good example for the kids, plain and simple. So what that she usually dressed a little more casually. Okay, make that a lot more casually. For today she wanted to be soft and flowing, even pretty. She embraced Skeeter's shoulders and sang the familiar hymn with soft, melodic gusto.

Craig knew Skeeter was in trouble before the unthinkable happened, but couldn't intervene quickly enough. Caught between family and friends, he watched the child's face wash pale. Trying to exit the narrow confines, he stepped on more than one foot, but to no avail. Before he could get her clear of the pew, Skeeter got sick, right on Sarah's pretty dress.

Pastor Weilers went silent. The congregation froze. A little girl groaned, then gagged in mockery or sympathy. An adolescent boy exclaimed, "Eeeeeuuuuwwww," in the loudest voice possible, while Brett and Olivia's mouths dropped open in disgust and embarrassment.

"I've got her." Craig hoisted the sick child. Mrs. Weilers bustled through the side entry, brandishing an armload of towels.

Numb, Sarah accepted the older woman's help as graciously as she could. The rank smell overshadowed the sweet mix of lemon oil and beeswax. Brett and Livvie headed out, humiliated. They'd escaped scot-free. The bulk of the mess had landed on Sarah, who held the lower edges of the skirt as she quietly fled the sanctuary. Mrs. Weilers followed, leaving pew cleanup to others.

"It should wash right out, this material being so good and all," she fussed outside, dabbing at Sarah's dress. Seeing how bad she felt, Sarah offered an apology.

"Would you tell the pastor how sorry I am for interrupting his homily? Please?"

"Sarah." The older woman brushed her concern off. "Everything in that church is washable. You take the little one and go home. Raising our three, this happened more than once, believe me. Ah, there they are." Mrs. Weilers dipped her chin toward the treed lot.

Craig reappeared, clutching Skeeter. Seeing the child's woeful expression, guilt swept Sarah.

She hurried across the lawn and held out her arms. Skeeter wept silent tears, a mix of chagrin and pain. "Hush, now. Hush. It's all right. We'll get you home, cleaned up and tucked into bed. Take care of that tummy." Crooning, she waited as Craig opened the truck door, then belted Skeeter in.

"I'll bring Liv and Brett," he told her, stepping back.

"Thanks. I can't imagine they want to ride with us at the moment." Climbing in, she refused to think how differently this trip had ended in her dreams. Accepting that with an equanimity she didn't feel, she cranked the window down and headed home.

"How's she doing?"

Sarah turned. Craig's concern was reflected in his face. "Better, but not ready to test the waters. And I'm okay with that."

He smiled. "I bet you are, though she only managed to get my shoe. You, on the other hand…"

"Don't remind me." Wrinkling her nose, Sarah looked around. "Where are Liv and Brett?"

"Unloading stuff. I stopped by the store to grab whatever we might need to take care of her."

Brett and Liv lugged in bags of gelatin, applesauce, Pedialyte and ginger ale. Sarah turned to Craig again. "Thank you."

"You're welcome. Want to shower?"

"Oh, yes."

"I'll watch her. Is she awake?" He peeked into the bedroom beyond the living room. "Nope. Out like a light. How about this," he posed, waving a hand to Brett and Livvie. "We'll make breakfast, and you take a nice relaxing shower. Soothe some of that tension away."

Until he said the words she hadn't recognized the strain.

She dropped her shoulders in gratitude. "Thanks. I won't be long."

"We're fine, Sarah." His tone and his look meant business. He nodded toward Livvie and Brett, and added, "Take your time."

She refused to think how badly this had turned out. Guilt ran roughshod over her for ignoring Skeeter's complaint, all because she had wanted to look nice for Craig Macklin in church.

Would she ever learn? Something about Craig made her common sense fly out the window while whims of imagination took root.

And why would he be interested, with their history and all?

Easy answer: he wasn't, but didn't want bad terms with his nearest neighbor. Or he was playing her like he played so many others, but that scenario boded certain disaster. Neighbors didn't need that kind of drama. She'd settle for back-door neighborly, a peaceful co-existence.

The man looked comfortable in her kitchen. Very comfortable.

Sarah swallowed hard, wishing he didn't look so at home.

He'd loosened his collar, rolled up his sleeves, and his tie was nowhere in evidence. The newspaper lay open on the counter. He read it while turning sausage and monitoring biscuits. The whole domestic scene brought to mind a host of possibilities that would have seemed impossible a few weeks before. Now?

Still impossible. Are you nuts? He's a Macklin, you're a Slocum. 'Nuff said. Still. "Hey."

He turned. Smiled. "You look beautiful."

Uh-huh. "Denim and easy-care knit, all the way."

He crossed the room and looked up. "You're as lovely now as you were walking into that church, Sarah. But nothing was as special as how you were coming out."

"Oh. Yes. Of course."

"I mean it." Craig met her gaze, unflinching. "You didn't come undone, didn't freak out. No yelling, cursing or whining. And you were a mess."

Oh, man. So this was how he attracted women? Are you kidding me? She made a face, doubtful. "Thanks for noticing."

"You focused on Skeeter," he reminded her. "So many women…" The sentence faded. He shook his head, thoughtful. "I've never met anyone like you, Sarah. All that strength and beauty." He extended his hand. She placed hers in it. He invaded her space, inhaled and smiled. "Meadow Romance."

"You remembered."

"Couldn't possibly forget."

She stepped ahead of him then turned and caught him appreciating the view. Her heart stutter-stepped and his frank grin made her feel young. Pretty. Totally out of character. She had no clue what to say or how to react. *Maintain a low profile. This guy's been around the block.*

"You're cooking? Really?"

"I said I would." He jutted his chin toward the stove. "You like your eggs scrambled?"

"Scrambled's good. Can I help?"

"Not 'til cleanup. If you refuse to buy a dishwasher, you'll be soaking your hands when I eat over, because I hate doing dishes."

Despite her internal admonition, her heart leapt at the promise to spend time with her. She slanted him a quiet look. "If you cook, I'll clean."

"Promise?"

His expression said he was two steps ahead of her in a game she'd never played. But she was beginning to like being on the board, letting the dice roll. "Promise."

Brett and Liv chattered throughout the brunch-time meal. Craig kept the conversation flowing, lightening the meal with humorous observations. It was a friendly time. Cozy. Family-oriented and normal.

Until Rita walked in and saw him sitting with her two kids.

Surprise gave way to dismay and embarrassment. Sarah stood. "Rita, you hungry?"

"No." Her expression said food ranked dead last on her list.

Craig rose as well. Brett and Liv went silent, their faces reflecting the grown-up strain.

"Craig made us breakfast," Sarah started to explain. "Skeet got sick at church—"

"She's sick?" Alarm replaced embarrassment. "With what?"

"A stomach bug," Sarah replied. "She's resting now."

"Why didn't you call me?"

Sarah hesitated, uncertain. For two years Rita had been literally out of the picture. The thought of calling her never crossed Sarah's mind. "I—"

"I better go." Craig eased past Rita. "Brett. Liv. Nice talking to you. And Sarah?"

She looked up. The look he sent her bolstered her confidence. "It's been nice."

She offered him a fleeting smile overshadowed by Rita's reaction. "Thanks for your help."

He smiled. "That's what neighbors are for."

Rita's gaze followed his progress down the driveway. "He's your neighbor? You're kidding, right?"

"No." Sarah answered slowly, reading Rita's expression. "He's building the house across the street."

Rita swore. Brett and Liv froze, then exchanged worried looks. Rita noted their movement, pressed her lips together and took a breath. "I have to call Kim."

Sarah gave her room to pass. "Skeet's in the front bedroom. She's been sleeping since we got home."

Rita showed no reaction. She took her cell phone outside, pressed a number down and proceeded to talk while Sarah and the kids tidied the kitchen. By the time she returned, Brett and Liv had disappeared.

"Rita, I'm sorry."

"For?"

"Not calling you. Having Craig here. Take your pick."

Rita sighed, her expression grim. "I'm not mad, Sarah. Not at you."

Sarah breathed a sigh of relief. "Then who?"

"Myself. I've been under the influence for a long time. Why would you even think to call me?"

True, but—"I should have, though. I will next time."

"And you can have anyone you want in your house," Rita continued. "It's your home. It just surprised me to see him here all comfy, cozy, chatting with my kids."

You and me both. Sarah nodded. "I understand."

Rita studied Sarah's face. Her look softened. "I know you do. I've spent years avoiding certain families because of what Tom did. I'm embarrassed to be around them. Guilt-ridden."

"But you did nothing wrong."

A sad smile curved Rita's mouth. "That's easy to say from where you're standing. From here?" Rita waved a hand to mark her stance. "Whole other thing. And you can't fix it for me," Rita warned. "I've got to toughen up, be able to handle this on my own. But it's no secret that people like Craig's grandfather might be alive today if it weren't for the strain of losing everything because of Tom's greed. And there are some who think I pushed him to it because I was high maintenance, accustomed to nice things. That's not an easy burden to bear."

"But it's not true," Sarah protested. "And you're getting better. Stronger, every day. I see it. The kids see it."

Rita shifted her look to the front window. The sound of a power saw meant Craig was hard at work. Her face shadowed. "I thought so too."

Chapter Sixteen

Sarah re-tied the bandanna around her forehead, wishing she hadn't lost her sweatband. Hay season was in full swing and working dawn to dusk in the heat of the late-June sun made a girl sweat.

She and the Bristols had been at it for days, first cutting and drying the alfalfa/timothy mix, then baling, moving and stacking. By the time they finished the task, a generous share of Maremma money would be spent in wages, but the barn would be stocked with winter food. A good cutting, too. Now, if the second cutting was as good or better—

Sarah focused on the job at hand. The meteorologists warned of late-day thunderstorms and there was still the west field to haul. How often had she watched farmers race the clouds, drawing piled-high, swaying hay wagons, scurrying for cover? Now she understood the need to rush, to protect the dried forage. Wet hay molded in storage, creating health problems. They'd gotten the first fields in. One to go.

The hard work kept her isolated. She hadn't seen much of anyone in the past two weeks, except the kids and Rita. With a deliberate frown she pushed away thoughts of her neighbor. She'd expected to see Craig with increased regularity now that Brett was helping him.

Nope. Not at all. Occasionally she'd see his SUV heading

into town or up his sloped drive, but the man himself? Not a thing. For two weeks.

Which was for the best, she counseled herself, nudging the feeling of warmth aside. Craig Macklin was off limits, despite the way her chest tightened in his presence. That should tell her something, she mused, her eye on the encroaching clouds. The edge of the front didn't look bad, but this low-pressure system had spawned tornadoes as far north as Michigan's Upper Peninsula. It packed heat. With the boys double-teaming the last hayfield, she should have everything under cover by late afternoon and a new pasture fenced by swinging three ends of the rotational fencing around, making her upper border the lower one. Moving the lightweight supports, she thanked God for the technology that made her Premier fence system woman-friendly.

Craig blinked, yawned, then peered into the microscope again. Yeah, there they were. Plain as day. Sarcoptic mange mites. No wonder Mrs. Ellers' young dog was uncomfortable. Frowning at the number of cases he'd seen of late, Craig planned the customary course of action, then moved back to the examining room to explain.

"So, she'll be okay?" Ava Ellers deep, lyrical voice put Craig in mind of Mississippi river boats. He nodded.

"Just fine. Typical infestation. We've seen a lot this year. Some pups are more prone than others."

"Well, that figures, doesn't it?" The coffee-skinned woman ran her fingers through the dog's curly ruff, her tone lightly scolding. "Skin mites, is it? Just keep them to yourself, little girl. I don't care to be scratching night and day like you've been doing." Turning concerned eyes back to Craig, she asked, "This will take care of it, Craig? I mean, Doctor?"

He laughed. He'd known the Ellers family forever. Mowed their lawn when he was in high school. Delivered their paper before that. Seeing Ava Ellers' calm smile reminded Craig of how far they'd come in three years. The Ellers family had invested big in Tom's plans. College funds, retirement. They'd gone under big time, just like Grams and Gramps, but time had erased their financial constraints.

"How's Jackie doing?"

"Well," Ava assured him, smiling. Their daughter's college education had been fully funded by a running scholarship.

"She did well at Nationals," Craig remarked. "Second in the women's three-thousand meter. Not too shabby."

"No, indeed." Ava smiled, pleased he'd kept track. "And the funny thing is, if we'd had the money to send her, she might not have worked so hard to run well. To win. Sometimes good comes out of bad in ways we least expect."

Her words nicked Craig's guilt bubble. Was it possible that good followed bad for a reason? A plan?

Of course not.

"I understand you've got Rita Slocum's boy helpin' you," Ava noted, her deep tones a wash of Southern elegance and backyard barbecue.

Craig's hands stilled. He acknowledged the truth with a slow nod. "Brett's a good kid. He needed something to keep him busy, so I—"

Ava stopped his litany by laying a soft, bronze hand on his arm. "There's no need to explain. That family is not responsible for the actions of the father. They are victims, same as us. Folks need to move on. Take care of their own."

"You're right." Craig nodded. "Sarah's had the kids with her while Rita's been—"

"Sick," Ava supplied, her eyes daring him to call it anything else. "Sarah's a good woman. Comes from good stock." She paused and shrugged. "In part, anyway. I knew her mama."

Craig quirked a brow of interest. "Did you?"

"Peg Slocum was a wonderful person. Tough, but kind. A true Christian who lived her faith. Sarah takes for her."

"It hasn't been easy." Craig thought of the weariness Sarah took pains to hide.

"No." Ava shook her head. "I don't suppose it has. But I think Sarah can handle whatever comes her way. She's strong. Faithful. She sent me a letter after that business with Tom, apologizing for her family's actions. And her no part of them, then shunned because she supported Rita."

Ava shook her head, eyes down, deep in thought. "Every year I read Barbara Robinson's *The Best Christmas Pageant Ever* to my class. They laugh at the antics of those Herdmans. The naughty things they did to those around them. When I read it?" She raised troubled eyes to Craig's. "I think Slocum."

"But not Sarah."

Ava smiled. "No. Not Sarah."

He hadn't seen his neighbor in two weeks. So what that he took comfort in her presence, wondering at the end of each busy day how hers had gone? How the pups were doing. But he stayed away, noting the temptation and willing to fight it for family comfort and Rita's state of mind. The pain that darkened her face when she found him sitting in Sarah's comfortable kitchen offered a harsh wake-up call. Rita had been through enough and her current hold was fragile. He had no right to mess with that.

That realization didn't stop him from thinking about Sarah on a regular basis. Okay. Make that constant.

Ava tilted her head. From the look in her eye, she read him with ease. Craig twitched a shoulder and narrowed his gaze. A smile edged Ava's mouth as she acknowledged his declaration. "No, you're right. Sarah's one of a kind."

Craig scanned the sky as he headed south from a Potsdam farm, then called Brett. "It's supposed to storm, Brett. We won't try to work tonight. Maybe you can help your aunt."

"Okay," Brett agreed. "She's moving fencing but got interrupted by the co-op guy. He wanted to pick up lambs a day early because of the holiday weekend, but forgot to tell her. Now she's got to hurry because it took us a while to gather the lambs."

Craig appraised the western sky. He noted towering cumulus, definitely storm material, but nothing out of the ordinary. That, he knew, could change. "Then you help her, Brett. She can't leave the fence half-done."

"Right. I will. 'Bye, Craig."

Uneasiness swept Craig.

He pushed it aside. Late-day thunderstorms were the norm once summer arrived. He'd seen Sarah and the Bristol boys running hay wagons the last few days. Made note of the long sleeves she wore despite the heat to protect her skin from the sharp-edged forage. He wanted to help, but the internal work on the house had to get done; to keep his costs down he needed to do some of the finish work himself. The longer days of June and July afforded him more time, but the influx of work had the vet clinic hopping. Throw Hank's vacation in for good measure and Craig had been working on short sleep for nearly twelve days. But Hank would be back after the Independence Day weekend, and Craig could slow down.

He hoped.

Sarah didn't need a watch to tell her that the hour-plus spent gathering lambs pushed her time frame. The wind had picked up. The air smelled of hot, sticky rain. The humidity weighted everything. Every so often the trees would still, their branches drooped and tired. Then the wind would roar once more and they'd dance in frenzied abandon, bending. Laughing.

The wire of the west side border twisted when the wind snatched it out of her hand. Sarah wanted to swear. And cry.

She did neither. Thinning her lips, she maneuvered the balance posts and wire back to their original position, aligning strands with a patience that would have made her tribal ancestors proud. Finally positioning the anchor posts to her liking, she stepped to the end. As she adjusted the prior side to meet and match the notches in the final curve, a crack of lightning split the air, its sound a sizzle. The thunder that followed was short moments behind. Sarah grimaced.

She wasn't afraid to get wet. Been there, done that. No big deal. But standing in an empty field in the middle of a thunderstorm was stupid.

No way could she outrun it. The initial gray cloud cover morphed to towering black cumulus, foreboding and ominous.

Lightning forked to the ground and danced from cloud to cloud in nature's own electrical parade.

Nor could she seek shelter from the nearby hedgerow. The trees were an obvious draw to the forked bolts.

Moving to the lower edge of the western fence line, Sarah spread the gate. A whistle brought Max. "Come bye, Max."

Circling clockwise, the black and white dog guided the free-ranging sheep to the open gate. "Good, good. Away, Max." Sarah kept her voice calm in spite of the electrically charged downpour.

The storm unnerved the sheep. It took Max long minutes and several tries to maintain the flock and move them along. With Molly by his side it would have been short work, but on his own the nervy sheep gave him trouble.

Sarah knew better than to interfere. It would only confuse the situation. Waiting it out with the wrath of Mother Nature crashing around her, she fought for patience.

A near strike sent her sprawling. Electricity sizzled in the wet grass beneath her. Knowing the ground was the safest place at the moment, she lay there, letting the storm beat around her as the dog worked the animals into the newly staked pen.

Tree branches snapped along the farm lane to her left. A maple sent a large limb down, the tearing wood an ominous sound. Keeping a low profile, Sarah moved to the gate as the last sheep entered and swung it shut with a sigh of satisfaction.

Thank You, God. Now, for home.

She turned, still crouched low, and gave Max leave to go. "That'll do, Max. Good dog."

She had no clue what happened next. One moment she was watching the tail end of the dog race for the barn and then sights and sounds combined to create a train-in-a-tunnel effect, the sound growing in strength and definition as she found herself smashed and tumbled into first the fencing, then a branch, then a thick-trunked tree.

Then nothing.

Chapter Seventeen

"Wow." Gazing out a north-facing window, Deb Macklin shook her head. "It looks wicked up your way, Craig."

Craig looked up from the newspaper and gave Rocket a lazy scratch. "Really?"

"Sky looks funny."

"We get storms all the time, Mom." Their eastern proximity left them wide open to nor'easters, and Canadian cold fronts never missed St. Lawrence County. Not as much snow as some lakeshore communities, but enough cold and wind to make a man sit up and take notice.

"Not like this." Deb frowned, obviously concerned, and Deb Macklin didn't get concerned easily. Craig rose.

"Craig?" Jim Macklin's voice hailed his younger son from the downstairs doorway.

"Yeah?"

"Grab the phone. Cade's trying to reach you but your cell is out."

Craig snatched up the landline. "What's up?"

"Trouble your way. The house looks okay from here—"

"Where's here?" Craig interrupted. From this angle he could see the roiling mass of clouds that banked north of his parents' lodge. "You at my place?"

"Sarah Slocum's. The kid found her lying unconscious in

a field. He couldn't move her, she was pinned under a large branch…"

"No." Craig's heart compressed in his chest and the cry was part prayer, part lament. He didn't try to hide the angst in his voice. "Where is she, Cade?"

"On her way to the hospital. The EMT figured her for a concussion, minimal. Her face is a mess, but vitals are good."

"Who's there?"

"You mean here? At the house?"

"At Sarah's." No way could Craig clamp down his anxiety. His voice went impatient. "Are the kids okay?"

"Brett's on the way to the hospital with her. The others are with Rita. It was just Sarah and the boy here."

"Dear God." Craig gripped the phone tighter, aware of his mother's attention, wondering why he hadn't followed his earlier instincts. If he'd been there—

He drew a deep breath and tried to calm his racing heart. Didn't work. "You're sure Sarah's all right?"

Cade's voice stilled. When he spoke again his voice was calm and measured, as though informing next of kin. "She's hurt. Significant. But not life-threatening."

"And the sheep?"

"I don't believe I'm having this conversation." Cade's tone deepened with curiosity. "I thought you hated sheep." Drawing a breath of interest, Cade continued, "She lost a bunch. By the way the hedgerow is twisted and mangled, Wynn figures a tornado finger-tipped the area. Sarah was arranging fencing when it hit. We've got some dead, some injured, and some placidly chewing their cud. Stupid things."

Craig grabbed his keys. "I'll stop at the clinic for supplies and get right over there. Call Hank, will you, since my cell's out? Fill him in. Have him meet me at Sarah's. And the Bristol boys," Craig added, his mind strategizing what they'd need to treat several hefty farm animals. "They can help shift the animals out of the field. I'll have Mom call Julie and Ralph. We've got to save what we can."

Visions of Sarah's hard work spun through his mind. Long

nights, bleating lambs. Every large animal vet understood the time and financial commitment that went into a new operation. It wasn't for the faint of heart, that's for sure. Yet Sarah had done it, single-handed, employing occasional part-time help to see her through. She'd done it and stood in the thick of a brutal storm to try and maintain it.

When he was through helping her, he might just throttle her himself. Save the next tornado the trouble.

Breathing hurt. The slightest movement of her lungs brought a knife-like burning to her ribs. Sarah tried to focus on the discomfort, like her mother taught her. Once centered, she would erect a mental shield against the pain. It was a skill that worked during those dark days following Peg's death. The days of just Old Tom and the boys, criticizing her. Ridiculing her every effort. Making her feel ugly. Stupid.

She might be able to draw on cultural strengths to block the physical pain, but the mental anguish didn't need stirring. Pushing it out of mind, she concentrated her efforts on what to do next. Open her eyes to face the damage or turn away from the pain and sink into oblivion?

Oblivion won.

The calm of the post-storm air infuriated Craig, acting meek and mild when less than an hour ago Mother Nature dumped fury on an innocent young woman and a flock of mindless sheep.

"Why, God?" he muttered as he packed the boot of the SUV, then hurried to the cab. Gravel spun as he directed the sleek 4x4 toward Waterman Hill. "Why Sarah? What has she done to deserve this? The girl lives her life to be kind and peaceful. Look what she had to overcome," he railed, temper mounting. "Born to a family that didn't appreciate her. Rejected by her father and brothers… Why pick on her?"

With a start Craig realized he was yelling as much at himself as his Savior.

Hadn't he judged Sarah? Spurned her? Just a few months

ago he'd been tempted to refuse her treatment because she was a Slocum.

He was as bad as the two Toms and Ed. Worse, because he'd been raised to be God-fearing. Not a presumptive, sanctimonious jerk.

Now here he was, barreling to her place, trying to help a woman he'd previously shunned.

How much had changed. His need to help her, protect her, was strong. He wasn't foolish. He understood the backlash. Grams didn't need constant reminders. Neither did Rita. And caring for Sarah brought his own guilt to the forefront constantly, her family a steady niggle of his own part in the whole mess.

"Feed my lambs." The Lord's admonition to Simon Peter came to him. *"Take care of my sheep."*

Three times Christ instructed a reinstated Peter to guard the flock, feed the sheep. The meaning was clear; Peter, forgiven for his lapse of strength and faith as Christ was beaten and scourged, was now given the command to guide the infant Church.

"God, I've got to tend these sheep now. Minister to them. I need to use my skills to save the work of Sarah's hands when I'd rather be with her. Keep watch on her, Father. Ease her pain, her suffering. Give her the gift of peaceful sleep; time for her body to heal. Take care of her."

Gone were any notions that God might be too busy to handle a personal entreaty. Craig's prayer was one-on-one, a direct line to Heaven.

He wheeled into her drive, scattering stone. The Bristol boys had helped move the remaining flock from the lower pasture. A caravan of trucks hauled the injured to the front barn. Hank jumped off the first pickup, his expression grim. "I've done the triage. There are some we can save, many we can't. Too much internal damage."

Craig trusted Hank. He knew the older vet would never take a farmer's loss lightly. Every breeding ewe was money in the bank to a sheep farmer. With no lambs to sell mid-fall,

Sarah's bank account would take a direct hit. And the time it took to rebuild a flock? How many more accounts would she have to keep by night just to stay afloat?

Hank jerked his head toward the barn. "Let's save the ones we can, ay? We've got a nice operating theater right here." The sound of wheels on gravel brought his head up. A look of satisfaction lightened Hank's eyes as he spied Julie's car with Ralph riding shotgun. "Now we're ready."

Twelve sheep saved. So few out of how many? Nearly thirty?

But it was a dozen more than Sarah would have had if the medical crew hadn't gathered. Jack and Mike Bristol agreed to stay the night, alternating watch. Once the cleft-hoofed patients were resting comfortably, Hank took Craig to the back pasture.

"That's where they found her."

"Where Brett found her."

Cade's voice came from behind. Craig turned and searched his brother's face for news. "Have you been to the hospital? How is she?"

"Asleep. She must have taken a full frontal into the tree before the storm dropped her to the ground. She'll be hurting."

"Did she say anything?" *Ask for me? Call for me?* While common sense told him there was no reason she should, he'd love to hear that she did. Cade shook his head.

"Nothing that made sense. Wynn said she whispered something about John being twenty-one, but he couldn't make sense of it."

"The concussion," Hank interjected. "They make you talk stupid. So, Sarah was here—" Hank waved a hand to the sugar maple that had been both torment and haven to the young farmer "—and the sheep were in this pasture."

The sight of the tree nearly gagged Craig, the huge branches lying haphazard on the ground. Their torn-away filaments looked stark and naked in the oblique evening light. Scattered along the sloped edge of the field lay the remains of nearly twenty sheep. The rumble of an approaching machine drew their attention. A backhoe approached, with old Ben Waters driving.

"I called him." Craig answered Cade's look of question. "I didn't want Sarah coming home to this. It'll be rough enough as it is."

"Good move." Cade's look said he heard more than Craig offered out loud. Ben stopped the big shovel and clambered down.

"Sorry business, boys." He stuck out a hand to greet each man, then angled a look to Craig. "Where shall I dig?"

"Here," answered Craig, then turned toward Sarah's bungalow, appraising the angle. "This will work. She won't be able to stare out the window and see it."

"Would Sarah do that?" Hank's voice said the woman he knew was too busy to dwell on the loss of a few sheep. But Craig had seen the exhaustion. The day-by-day struggle of kids, sheep, land, accounts and Rita.

"We won't give her a chance," he replied, wanting to kick himself for his self-imposed exile these past two weeks. If only…

"Craig's right," offered Cade, surveying the sight. "Sarah's had a lot on her plate. No call to add to it. The fencing's shot."

The remains of the tension-wired fence lay knotted and tangled. "We'll get rid of that tomorrow," promised Craig. He glanced at his watch. "Hank, I'm heading to the hospital. You're okay here?"

"Fine. I want to recheck our patients before I leave. Go over the instructions with Jack and Mike."

"Thank you." Craig grasped his partner's hand. "I appreciate you coming right out."

Hank shrugged. "Part of the job."

"I mean it." Craig met Hank's eye. "And whatever's owed from this, we'll take from my account." The veterinary practice kept employee accounts for animal care.

Hank paused, then nodded. "Whatever you say, Craig."

Cade gave Ben a hand up to the raised seat of the hydraulic shovel. Once Ben was resettled, he turned to Hank. "I'll help Ben. You might want to send Jack to help move the bodies once the hole's dug."

"I'll do that." Hank's eyes scanned the field, littered with dead ewes. "Rough day for our little shepherd."

Craig heard the remark, but kept his eyes averted as he climbed into the SUV. All too easily it could have been Sarah lying there, still and broken on the rich, green grass. Try as he might, he couldn't push the thought aside. He could have lost her before he had a chance to know her. At this moment, arguments about family feelings seemed inconsequential compared with the thought of losing Sarah for good. He scowled as he pulled away, heading toward the hospital.

He'd gotten something many wish for and never receive. A wake-up call, a second chance.

Craig was ready to take it.

Chapter Eighteen

Murmured voices almost brought Sarah to the surface. She listened with care for one certain voice, sure to recognize the low, gentle timbre beneath the others.

It wasn't there. Quiet re-descended as she shifted away from the pain, remembering the crush of the tree pressing her into the rain-slicked ground.

"Sarah Slocum's floor?"

A pink-smocked woman nodded.

"How is she?" Craig continued, his medically trained mind jumping to worst-case scenarios.

"Are you next of kin?"

"A friend."

"Craig." Brett's voice interrupted them from behind.

Craig turned. Brett barreled toward him, offering explanation, his step awkward. "I couldn't get it off her. I tried. I really did. It wouldn't budge."

Pain and guilt weighted Brett's features. Craig hugged him hard, the boy's tears dampening Craig's shirt. "Your mother here?"

Brett nodded and pulled back. Snuffling, he wiped his nose on the upper edge of his T-shirt. "She's with Aunt Sarah, but they won't let her do anything."

Craig frowned. "What do you mean?"

"Aunt Sarah won't wake up and they wanted permission to do some tests, but Mom can't give it."

"Where's the doctor?"

Brett nodded behind Craig. "That's him."

Craig did an about face. "Excuse me."

The doctor raised his head, his look moving from Craig to Brett and back. "Yes?"

"You're treating Sarah Slocum?"

An eyebrow rose. "Yes."

"I understand you have questions about tests. Procedure."

The doctor looped his stethoscope around his neck and nodded. "She hasn't come to. Early tests show some internal blood loss. Ideally, we need permission to scope her. Do an exploratory."

"Ideally?"

The doctor's brow rose higher. "If medically necessary we'll go ahead and perform the procedure. It's just better to have our I's dotted and T's crossed."

"But you won't hesitate to do what's necessary, right?" Craig drove the point home. "Sarah would want you to do whatever should be done."

The doctor's look changed to one of understanding. "It's hard before you're married, isn't it?" he mused, moving down the hall.

Craig darted a glance toward Brett as they kept pace, the boy's face half frown, half curious. "No, I—"

"I understand completely." The middle-aged doctor waved a sympathetic hand. "It's medical no-man's land. Legally, you've got no rights. Morally, you have every right to permit treatment of the woman you love."

Brett's attention shifted back to Craig. The doctor swung open the door to Sarah's room. "Now, if Sleeping Beauty wakes up, we can end the suspense. Have her sign her own papers. Give it a try, Prince Charming. Maybe your voice will bring her around."

Rita stood in front of the bed. She looked startled to see

him. Liv and Skeeter sat in tandem on a chair at the end. Reading their faces, Craig knew this wasn't the time to correct the M.D. He moved forward. Rita stepped aside.

His heart jerked at the sight of Sarah. The monitors and IV tubing didn't jolt him. The sights and sounds of technical intervention were commonplace at the clinic, although his patients were generally hairier. And four-footed.

Her face had taken the brunt of the trauma. Swelling obscured her warm, round eyes. Cuts and lacerations vied with angry bruising for surface area. If he hadn't been told this was Sarah, he wouldn't have known. Easing onto the bed, he called her name.

No response.

Gentle, he lifted her hand, his thumb caressing the palm, trying to stimulate her with the basest sense, touch. Again he called her name.

Nothing.

The doctor shrugged. "Concussion. We'll do what we have to without consent if it comes down to it. She's got no parents? No brothers or sisters?"

Craig looked at Rita. She stared back at him, then lowered her eyes. They both understood that Sarah's father and brother would be in no hurry to stop by. "Her father's local. And her brother, Ed."

The doctor's brows drew together. "The car dealer on Cable 8?"

You mean the moron on Cable 8. "Yeah."

"They know about this?" The doctor turned Rita's way.

Shame and worry vied for top billing. "They know. They won't come."

Craig muttered something not pretty. The doctor's face said he understood their anger. "Someone will stay with her?"

"Yes," promised Craig.

"Yes," offered Rita. Their simultaneous response inspired a shared look of concern. Craig met the doctor's eye. "One of us will be with her. Rest assured."

"Then I'll be back later," the doctor said.

"Well." Craig stared at Sarah, his medical mind envisioning the pain involved with her facial injuries. "I'm glad she's sleeping."

Rita sighed. "Me, too. It's got to hurt so much." Her long, slim, tapered fingers gripped the coverlet. Craig noticed she wore no ring. Funny. A few days ago that might have brought him satisfaction, the idea that she'd moved beyond her marriage to Tom, Jr.

Now it didn't matter. The only thing that had meaning was getting Sarah better. Helping her heal.

"Listen! Look! Here he comes, leaping across the mountains, bounding over the hills..." The snip from the second chapter of Song of Songs danced in Sarah's head. Peace flooded her, leaving her breathless. Her hands fluttered, searching for something, someone.

A strong hand captured hers, the masculine touch tender and firm. A nice mix. "It's all right, Sarah. Everything's all right. Sleep."

Her heart rate slowed. Her hands eased their frantic pawing. His voice brought safety and comfort. Relaxing, she felt the gentle pressure of his hand and the comfort of his presence.

She slept.

As morning sun brightened the elongated windows, Craig felt a slight shift beneath his fingers. "Hey. You waking up?" Half standing, he leaned over the bed, keeping his touch light.

She moaned, a heart-wrenching sound. Craig cringed. His gut ached. A tear trickled out of her right eye. Gentle, he brushed it away, torn between encouraging the wakefulness and its accompanying pain or letting her drift back to sleep. Her vitals were stable. While sleeping, she wasn't cognizant of the damage she'd suffered. Awake would be a whole different story.

An incoming nurse made the decision for him. "Waking up, I see. Hello, dearie. How are we doing?"

The inane question tweaked Craig's ire. One look at Sarah's

face showed how she was doing. Disregarding his frown, the nurse bustled about. "You've got a fine young man here, don't you? Been here some hours now." With hands that were not nearly as careful as his had been, the nurse checked Sarah's vitals. "And you're doing as well as can be expected after your little mishap, hey? How're you feeling, girlie?"

Sarah winced. Craig gripped her hand, offering support. Her mouth moved with effort, the words indistinct. "Don't... call...me...that. Please."

He leaned closer. "What? What did you say, Sarah?"

Eyes shut tight, she worked her jaw, grimaced in pain, ran her tongue around her lips, and said, "Don't call me girlie."

The nurse inclined her head. "Then I won't," she declared. "Just an expression, you know, but I can call you other things. How about..."

"Sarah."

Craig sagged in relief. That sounded like the girl he knew. He met the nurse's eye. "It's a great name."

"Well, it is, and don't I know it, my granny's name and all. Not one of us inherited her name, can you believe it? Seven children, five of them girls, and not a Sarah among 'em. Now, my second-born, she's a Sara, without the H, you know, more modern and all, and a university girl in Albany."

"That's nice." Craig replied, then nodded toward the bed. "But this Sarah needs more rest."

"Aye, but it's good to see her waking a bit, coming to and all. They worried sick for her when they brought her in, her face torn up like that. I bet she was a pretty thing, wasn't she?"

"Go," Craig ordered, half standing, his palms braced against the arms of the chair. He put on his doctor's voice, not bothering to soften the anger at her thoughtlessness. Without ceremony he pointed to the door. "Out."

"Why—" Flustered, the middle-aged woman looked flummoxed, then reared back realizing what she'd said. "I meant nothing by it. Just a shame and all."

Craig stepped away from the chair. The nurse beat a hasty

retreat, hands waving. A long moment of silence ensued before Sarah asked, "How bad is it?"

His hesitation told her more than his words. "It looks worse than it is. Probably feels that way, too."

"There's a comfort."

Her tone told him she was erecting walls faster than he could possibly dismantle them. "You broke your cheekbone and your nose. Loosened a few teeth. Some cuts and bruising. Facial edema, typical with your injuries. They've applied ice and they have you on an IV antibiotic laced with pain meds. There's bruising across your chest and upper arms, but no broken ribs or punctured lungs. Once the swelling goes down, they'll realign the cheekbone. Six weeks healing time, more or less."

"So I'm grotesque and snaggle-toothed." She kept her eyes closed, her tone defeated. "Go home, Doctor."

"Once Rita's back, I'll head to the clinic."

"Reet was here?" Her tone brightened. Rita's presence obviously made her happy. His? Not so much.

"She took the kids home late last night. We're taking shifts."

"Yours is over."

"And you're testy. I've had mutts with better temperament after a car chase gone bad. Lay off, Sarah."

"Craig…"

He ran one finger along the curve of her less-injured cheek. "I'm so sorry you got hurt. I wish I'd been closer. There to help."

Her cheek arched into his touch. Not much, but the reaction sent a more defined signal to a man who'd just been ordered out of the room. Maybe his attentions weren't as unwelcome as the young shepherd made out.

"How are the sheep?"

He drew a breath. "Sixteen were lost. We saved twelve." He watched while she digested the information. Saw her lip quiver before she clamped it down. "I'm sorry."

"Me, too."

The doctor strode in. "The princess awakens. How are we doing?"

"My face and chest met a sugar maple head on. I've been better."

"Feisty." The doctor made a note. He eyed Craig. "Is this normal behavior or out of the ordinary?"

"Depends who she's talking to, I'd say."

"Oh." Another note scribbled. "Pain, Sarah?"

"No, thanks. I've got plenty."

"Sarah." Her responses unnerved Craig. Calm, strong, stoic Sarah Slocum was in rare form. The doctor nudged Craig's shoulder. He looked up.

"Pain meds can render a normally quiet person quite talkative. Even combative. Could be what you're seeing."

"Either that or someone has taken over her body," Craig replied with a shake of his head. "Normally Sarah's more reticent."

"And you know this because...?" Her right eye peeked open, glaring. He drew his brows together, made his look quizzical.

"Love thy neighbor, Sarah." He ignored her huff of indignation. "Straight out of the Bible."

"A recent acquaintanceship?"

That arrow hit home. Craig shrugged it off. "Let's say an old friend, revisited."

"Go find your model girlfriend, Doc. She fits your style."

"She doesn't." Something in his tone snared her attention. She stared at him, vulnerable. Once more he ran his forefinger along the edge of her cheek. "My style's more classic."

"This week." Cynicism laced her tone. Craig glanced left as the door swung open. Rita entered, an eyebrow up.

"Maybe next week as well," Craig teased, keeping his finger gentle beneath her cheek. "Rita's just come in, which means I have to go to work." He stood, stretching. "Great chair." His frown said it was anything but.

The doctor nodded. "I'm going to talk with our patient. Because the zygoma is a painful break, I'm going to keep her on meds until the throbbing lessens and the swelling reduces. The maxillofacial surgeon should be around later today. Sarah's rate of healing will decide the surgery schedule. Luckily, the nose break was at the bridge and has aligned itself perfectly so we shouldn't need reconstruction there as long as it heals in position."

"Good." Craig leaned down, angling his head to catch Sarah's averted gaze. She shut her eye, blocking him out. He squeezed her hand. "I'll be back later. Behave."

Nothing. He rolled his eyes at her bad-temperedness and faced Rita. "All yours."

Rita shook her head. "I've never seen her like this," she whispered, eyes wide. "Sarah can make it through days without uttering more than a handful of sentences. And she's always the peacemaker."

"Either I bring out the worst in her—" watching Sarah's face, Craig noted the wince "—or the meds have her high."

"Oh."

Rethinking his choice of words, Craig cringed. Saying "high" to an alcoholic might be insensitive.

Rita read his look. "It's a feeling I've some experience with," she noted, wry, an eyebrow arched in his direction.

Heat climbed Craig's neck. He fumbled for words. Rita laid a hand on his arm, her look gentle. "It's fine, Craig. Go to work. I've got her."

He nodded and turned once more to the bed. "I'll be back later. And I'll check on the sheep. Jack and Mike are taking care of things."

No answer. Craig sighed and headed for the door. She called his name as he reached for the handle. He stepped back. "Yes?"

"Thank you."

His heart lightened. He gripped the edge of the door, knuckles straining, and gave her a slow nod she couldn't see. "You're welcome, honey."

Chapter Nineteen

Honey? Honey? Through the clench of pain, Sarah's anger surged. How dare he? How—

Alongside the anger sparked a flash of hope. A hint of peace inspired by the graze of his finger against her skin. The comfort it inspired, and the longing that rose within.

He'd do the same for someone's dog, she scolded, tamping the rise of expectation. *Don't fool yourself that anything's changed. Craig Macklin knows the moves of a game you've never played. Adjust your books accordingly, girl.*

Pushing thoughts of Craig aside, she focused her good eye on the doctor. By the time he finished road-mapping treatments, waves of sleep pressed upon her like a quilted throw. As the doctor's footsteps faded, Rita came into her viewing space. In one hand she clutched a travel mug of coffee. The other gripped a book. She held them aloft. "Sleep," she ordered, her voice sounding like the Rita of old. "I've got a great book and twenty ounces of premium coffee. I'm good to go."

Sarah blinked, trying to focus, but her eyelids refused to stay open. Rita gave her a gentle smile. The hand that smoothed hair away from her forehead was tender but strong. "Sleep, Sarah. I'll be here when you wake up."

* * *

Drifting between the lure of the muted afternoon sun and the veil of med-induced sleep, Sarah mulled her situation.

She'd listened for his voice. During the hours of fighting pain and losing, she'd listened, hoping to hear him call her name.

Then she woke to find him sitting with her. Holding her hand. It made her blush to remember her reaction to his touch. The thrill his interest inspired.

Disciplining herself, she drew to mind every blank look Craig ever threw her way, every slight she could remember. That should give her enough backbone to resist Dr. Macklin's newly enthused attentions. Memories of the strawberry blonde in the silver coupe were icing on the cake. Craig was a player.

Sarah was fresh out of games.

She'd slept most of the day. Rita appeared to be enjoying the almost finished book. She even gave an exaggerated glance to her watch once Sarah woke. "You can rest more, you know. I've got seventy pages left so another hour's nap would be just fine."

"Was that a joke?"

"Kind of."

"Nice improvement, Reet. You got another?"

"Aren't you tired?"

"Been sleeping all day." Sarah remembered the disjointed dreams, the waxing feeling of loss of control. "What time do I get my pain meds again?"

"That bad, huh?" At Sarah's blink, Rita shook her head and waved a hand to the IV. "You're getting them, doll face. Right there. They're pumping steady."

"Not enough."

Rita started to commiserate but Sarah waved her off. "Ignore me, Reet. I don't know what I'm saying half the time. Things I'd never normally say out loud come shooting out of my mouth."

"Then this could be an interesting night."

Sarah turned her head with care. Craig lounged in the doorway, a bouquet of flowers clutched in his hand. He moved forward, his gaze locked on hers. At the bed he handed them to her, watching as she brought the mixed bunch to her nose. She took a deep breath, enjoying the blend of fragrances, spicy and sweet.

"Like 'em?"

She swallowed hard, not looking up. "They're beautiful."

"I thought so." Craig leaned in for his own sniff. "They had all kinds," he explained, his voice gentle. His proximity made it impossible not to look at him. Gold eyes flecked with brown, clean-shaven, thick brows that matched his sandy hair. The smell of fresh soap and nice aftershave with a hint of coffee. A heady combination. "Roses. Daisies. Some cool, tropical-looking thing with a name that rivals medical terminology." He paused, watching her. "I thought a mixed bouquet was best."

"Because I'm a mix." Sarah knew her tone was defensive. She didn't care.

"Aren't we all?" Staring her down, he continued, "I was thinking more along the lines of personality." He fingered a sturdy yellow mum. "Strength." His eye went to a magnificent rose. "Beauty." He shifted his gaze to a fresh, white daisy. "Endurance." Bending, he inhaled the scent of a gorgeous lily. "And faith. It reminded me of you."

Rita stood. "Craig, I'm heading out since you're here. I'll bring the kids back later. I told Sarah I'm moving in to her place for a bit. Help take care of things until she can do it herself. I'm sure the idea totally intimidates her." Giving her sister-in-law a grin, Rita turned back to Craig. "But it will make things easier all around."

Craig nodded. "I think it's a great idea."

Sarah snorted. "Who asked your opinion?"

Craig met Rita's eye over the flowers. "Still feisty?"

"Oh, yeah."

"We could up the meds." He studied the IV, pondering. "Can't be much different from a canine hookup. I just adjust this little valve here—"

"That's not funny." Sarah stared up at him, her gaze a mix of humor and consternation.

"Then behave yourself," Craig ordered mildly, holding her look. Reading the intensity there, she glanced down. Gulped. He arched his left brow. "That's better. We're going to employ a new rule for the rest of the night. If you can't say something nice—"

"I've got it." Adjusting her body with care, Sarah slid down to rest, avoiding his look. "Thanks for coming, Reet. For staying."

Glancing from one to the other, Rita couldn't hide the smile tugging at her mouth. "He's being awfully nice, Sarah. Cut him some slack, okay?"

Sarah grunted, face turned. Meeting his gaze made it difficult to keep her distance. Maintain her necessary barriers.

Rita puffed out a breath. "I'll see you later."

"Love you, Reet."

Rita smiled, giving Sarah a carefully placed kiss. "Love you, too. I'll be praying for fast healing, Sarah. And an open mind."

Sarah groaned. "Stick to the healing, thanks. I've got the rest under control."

Rita's gaze flicked from Sarah to Craig and back again. "Right."

"You're still here?" Half asleep, her voice didn't sound nearly as cantankerous. Craig leaned forward.

"Yup."

"Don't you need to go home? Get some sleep? Change?" Her gaze traveled the length of him, noting his outfit.

"Hank ran the clinic this afternoon so I could grab a nap and clean clothes." His glance down indicated his blue jeans. "These are definitely a deeper blue than last night's. Can't you tell?"

"Last night?" Her voice bordered dreamy. "I don't remember much of last night, Doc."

Good, he thought, imagining the pain her mind intentionally blocked. He nodded. "Perfectly understandable. You slept the night away. And the day, from the sound of it."

"I was tired." Her sleepy glance fell on the bouquet now snugged in a water-filled vase. "The flowers. I almost forgot. They're beautiful, Craig."

First name basis again. He hid a smile. One step forward, two steps…

He smiled at her, squeezing her hand and made small talk while the evening nurse checked Sarah's vitals. "I stopped by your place this afternoon. The Bristols are doing fine. Rita's going to take her suitcase over there tonight. Get settled. I know it will be noisy, but Brett knows the routine and Rita can easily run the house for you. Besides, it will keep her busy. Focused."

Sarah nodded, unable to speak around the thermometer.

"The sheep were doing okay today?" she asked when the nurse had recorded her temperature.

"Better," he acknowledged. "We're watching the injured ones for spontaneous abortion, but we still had solid heartbeats today."

"Good." She angled her head, offering him a better view of the less injured side.

"Don't do that," Craig protested, leaning forward. "You don't have to turn your face away. It doesn't bother me." The look his words inspired made him squirm. "No, wait, I mean it bothers me that you got hurt." Agitated, Craig narrowed his eyes and ran a hand across his hair. "It doesn't bother me that your face is—" He muttered something under his breath, then faced her square. "I don't know how to say this and make it come out right."

Sarah's heart squashed like a puffed marshmallow oozing out the sides of a s'more. "I understand."

"Do you?" His expression was earnest, his eyes tired. She nodded.

"Yes. The surgeon was by this afternoon."

"What did he say?"

"How incredibly sexist."

"He said I'm incredibly sexist?" Craig grinned, misreading her with intent. "I don't even know him and already he's a fan."

"He's a she," Sarah remonstrated. She started to shake her head at him, but the pain reminded her it wasn't the best of ideas. "She said I'll be looking at surgery in approximately two weeks time. Then about six weeks for the bone to heal."

"Pretty much what we figured." Craig drew up her hand. He plied the fingers gently. "The pain's a little better, I take it?"

She glanced down at their linked hands. "How can you tell?"

"First, you're not reaming me continually. Second—" he grinned at the expression on her face "—your fingers are relaxed. When you're in pain, breathing accelerates, muscles tighten and hands tense. Loose fingers are a sign of less pain." Once more he smiled, but this time his eyes traveled to her mouth before making a tug-boat slow trip back to her eyes.

She leaned against the pillow and watched him. He smiled, raised her hand, and kissed the telltale fingers. "I think we'll let your face heal a bit more before we attempt anything else, Miss Slocum."

She snatched her hand back, ignoring the shot of pain into her shoulder. "You're cocky."

"Yeah." He gave her a lazy smile, then yawned. "And tired. Mostly tired."

"Go home," she told him, glancing to the window. "Catch up on your sleep. Rita will be by soon." She should have left it at that. She knew it, but couldn't resist adding, "There's really no reason for you to be here."

His eyebrow quirked. The grin went from lazy to mischievous in a flash. "None?"

"No." She wished she felt as sure as she sounded.

He leaned forward. The scent of soap and spice drifted with him, assailing her senses once again. Enticing her. Tempting her forward. "Nothing comes to mind?"

"No." That refusal was a little less confident, perhaps.

"Not a clue?" He leaned down until his face was just above hers, his eyes warm, his mouth curved in a teasing grin. Once again his eyes slid to her mouth. She felt a shiver of promise. A yearning to move toward him. Ease the distance.

"Not really…" Oh, man, that one sounded lame even to her. Spineless. Disconcerted.

Leaning farther, Craig pressed gentle lips to her temple. "Then we'll have to work on that."

"I—we—"

Craig placed a finger to her lips. "Shh. You sound tired, too. Maybe it's time for another nap."

A nap sounded safe. Staring at him, she slid down again with careful movements. With a sigh she sank her good cheek into the softness, welcoming its presence. "They said I can go home tomorrow."

His voice was gentle and low. "Good."

"Rita will come for me."

"Then I'll see you at home."

"Brett will be there. He'll see to things." She'd come to lean on the boy's capabilities more and more these last weeks. He was a willing student and a fast learner. They could get by without Craig's help.

"I have to visit the sheep. Check on their care."

"Oh. Of course." Duh, Sarah. He was a vet and lived right across the street. She was an animal owner. It behooved Craig to stay on her good side when she had so many potential patients, even though he'd probably rather have Hank oversee the care of her flock.

She knew how he felt about sheep. She knew how he felt about lots of things. Steeling herself, she tried to remember Craig's face when he'd spurned her. When he'd overlooked her deliberately, time and again.

This time she couldn't. The only image she conjured was a more recent variety. His eyes warm and caring, his smile tender. Man, she must be on drugs.

She was on drugs. That nudge of realization almost brought a smile.

She was medicated, no doubt about it. Her biggest fear was that Craig Macklin would still look this good once the meds were discontinued. Then what was she supposed to do?

Chapter Twenty

Walking past the impromptu gravesite two weeks later, Sarah fought a wave of sadness. The long, earth-covered hole offered silent testimony to the forces of nature. It was a reminder of keen loss, her fall market lambs dead and buried, and the ewes, such gentle creatures.

Her surgery was scheduled for the morning. Sarah considered the prospect with mixed feelings. The unsightly mess of her face needed attention, the sooner the better. She hated what she'd become, a living Greek drama mask, split down the middle, one side misshapen, the other almost normal. The rare glimpse she caught brought back every insult Tom and Ed had ever hurled her way.

The idea of metal pins and plates in her cheek upset her. She tried to ease her worry by starting a project at the wheel, spinning Icelandic fleece into a two-ply skein, but couldn't lose herself in the softness of the wool. Thoughts crowded, interrupting the peaceful movements of the treadle and the rhythmic pull and twist of the carded fibers.

She knew the surgery was a relatively simple procedure. The surgeon was confident and competent. She'd addressed Sarah's fears, answering questions in a direct manner.

But she saw the outside Sarah, the calm, secure, self-controlled Abenaki woman. No one saw the girl within, the child who'd been called homely too many times to count.

"You break that mirror yet, Ugly?" Ed's voice haunted her, taunting.

"Ed, you need to be politically correct," Tom Jr. cautioned, mock-serious. *"She's not ugly. She's 'appearance challenged.'"*

Ed had raised his green glass longneck in salute. "That sounds real nice, Tom. Educated."

Tom shrugged. "Just prettying up the facts."

The pre-adolescent Sarah ignored them, just as she had all the times before. It angered the brothers when their cheap shots made no overt impression on her. They behaved all right when her mother was around. While Peg lived, even Old Tom had shown her some respect and affection. Nothing you'd call love, but Sarah was fairly sure that was in short supply in Slocum assets. Her mother's steady presence and faith offered a shelter of normalcy in an otherwise dysfunctional family. When Peg died, Sarah's safety net died with her. By then, Tom and Ed were grown and gone, leaving their attacks to the occasional visit, but it was enough to make a girl question the reflection in the mirror and find it wanting.

Or just plain ugly.

"There you are." Spotting Sarah as he rounded the corner of the back barn, Craig saw the pained look, the troubled frown. He tried not to notice as she shifted her face, gazing outward, offering him a view of the less injured side. "Hank sends his best. His wife sent a pound of maple-walnut fudge. I snagged a little and set it aside because the ravenous adolescent vultures in your kitchen circled as soon as I approached the back door."

"They're always hungry," she agreed, still not looking at him. "Between Bonnie's kindness and Rita's baking, we'll be needing a diet."

Craig cast her an encompassing look, his appraisal disagreeing. "Nothing wrong with the view from where I'm standing."

Sarah frowned. Her glance flitted up, then down, in uncharacteristic fashion. She started for the barn.

"Worried about tomorrow?" Craig fell into step beside her, matching her pace. While she was much better, he knew she winded easily, her body protesting its rough treatment at the hands of the freak storm. "I'll pick you up at six."

"Rita's taking me." Her voice left no room for argument.

"Then I'll meet you there."

Sarah inhaled on a sharp note. Her shoulders stiffened. She looked about to cry and he wished she would. Maybe a good bawling session would release the trapped feelings. She turned, abrupt. "There's no reason for you to be there. I don't want you there."

It took effort to hide the effect of her words, but Craig managed it. "You're angry. Maybe a little depressed after all that's gone on. It doesn't hurt to have friends at a time like this."

"We're not friends," she retorted, heading for the stall that held the Border collie pups. "You ostracized me for a long time, Craig, making me feel guilty for something I had no control over. My genes. My family. Well, let me tell you something, Doctor." She spun about, nailing him with her gaze. "I don't need your friendship or your pity. I've made it through a lot of years without the blessing of Craig Macklin. I guess I can make it through another day."

"Sarah, I—"

"You don't get it, do you?" Her voice rose, disconcerting the little dogs. "Maybe you've smartened up. Gotten a clue. Well, that's great. Wonderful. I'm so very inspired by your change of heart." Her voice went hard and sarcastic. "But it's a one-way street, Doc. I've been scorned and ridiculed by experts in the field, so it's not like I'm unaccustomed to the feeling." Her dry honesty wrenched his heart. "But I'm not inclined to self-degradation. Or forgiveness at the moment."

He took a step back, regarding her, hands out in placating fashion. "You shouldn't go into surgery all riled up like this. There's a prayer service tonight at Westside Community. Maybe you and Rita could go." He took another step in retreat.

She turned her back on him, intent on the pups, her mouth compressed, her profile stern. Knowing she should go under anesthesia with a calm mindset, he walked to the barn door, standing half-in, half-out. "If you need me, I'll be around. You've got my cell number."

Silence answered him. He pawed at a driveway stone with the toe of his boot, then stepped fully through the door. "Good night, Sarah."

Prayer service. Right. Spurn a man's lame attempts at reconciliation and right away you must be in need of prayer. Supplication. While Sarah cleaned the collie stall, the little female that sought Craig's attention on a regular basis batted her boot with a disgruntled paw, as if wondering why she'd sent him away.

Why, indeed? *Because I'm hideous*, Sarah thought, unable to push the reality out of mind. She eyed the pup that thought chasing boot-clad feet a wonderful game, although it made raking the dirty shavings difficult. After stepping on the pup a second time, Sarah scooped her up. "Stop. You need to stay over here," she scolded, tucking the pup into a closed-in corner.

"I know," she acknowledged, seeing the pup gaze woefully toward the door. "I sent him off and you wanted some time with him. But it does you no good to set your sights on someone like that, young lady. There are plenty of beautiful dogs out there..." At the pup's vexed look, Sarah righted her words. "I mean other beautiful dogs, of course." Stroking the saddle-backed collie, Sarah met her eye-to-eye.

"We're not his type, little lady. Especially now," she explained to the pup, glancing at her distorted reflection in the barn window. "Even if we were, he..." Thinking aloud, Sarah raised her eyes, staring out the front barn door in direction of Craig's unfinished home. "He deserves beauty. Maybe craves it." Her gaze wandered the visible corner of his house, the stately country bearing of the extended Cape structure. It rose from the hillside in pristine splendor, cream on cream, the gray and red stone of the chimney adding warmth and color, accenting the deep berry tones of the shutters. "He's not for us."

"Sarah?" A voice from the side door brought her head around.

"Mr. Shackles." Blushing, Sarah's look went from him to the dog and back again. "I was talking to the pup."

He nodded, his glance noting the emptiness of the barn. "I was wondering," he admitted. He indicated the stone drive behind him. "I've got something for you. From the missus and myself."

Sarah stepped through the barn door and spotted a pair of sheep in the boot of Floyd Shackles' truck. Turning, she furrowed her brow. "I don't understand."

"They're all up to date," he rambled, unhooking the tailgate latch. "You can separate them if you want, but they haven't been exposed to anything. And their testing is negative."

"But I—"

Floyd unloaded the pair of sheep. "Dorset/Finn, just like the rest of yours. When we saw how well you were doing with the STAR program, all on your own, Betty and I just up and kicked ourselves. 'If a little girl like Sarah Slocum can work the accelerated program, why can't we?' the missus says. And I see she's right, so we buy some new sheep and these two are from our first breeders. What do you think?"

"They're beautiful." Gently, Sarah smoothed the short coats of the ewes. "Did you bring them to show me what you'd done?" Turning, she lifted her gaze to his.

Floyd shook his head. "No ma'am. They're for you. We felt bad at your loss and know how hard you've worked to put this place together. We see the lights, nights on end. We just wanted to say we're sorry you got hurt. Lost your flock."

"Mr. Shackles—"

"Floyd."

"Floyd, this is kind of you, but—"

"Well, now, the missus won't be hearing any buts." The man's voice toughened in that distinction. "When she takes to kindness, she's not one to take no for an answer. I'm smart enough not to buck her, Miss. I think you'd be wise to do the same. Best be on, now. She'll be waiting supper."

"Mr. Shackles. Floyd…" Sarah fumbled for words. Then she looked into the faded, sea-green eyes of the old farmer and relented. "Thank you, sir. And Betty as well. I'm grateful."

"Well, then." He huffed a bit, then rolled his shoulders. "Betty will be glad to hear it. She'll come around soon, no doubt. Bring you more of her fresh bread."

"I'll look forward to it, sir." Biting back words of argument, Sarah extended her hand. "God bless you."

"And you." The old man grabbed her hand in a gnarled paw. "You do good over here." He directed a general nod to the farm as a whole before he climbed into the seat of his pickup. "Hope your operation thing goes okay tomorrow."

Sarah nodded, having no idea how Floyd Shackles knew she was scheduled for surgery. "Thank you. I'm sure it will be fine. Nothing major, you know." For some reason, saying the words out loud brought comfort.

"Glad to hear it." The old man headed down the drive with a nod and a wave. Sarah eyed the pair of freshened ewes before her.

"Well, girls. Let's find a spot for you, shall we?"

Once she had the ewes sequestered, Sarah went in search of Rita. "I'd like to go to the service tonight at Westside Community. Care to join me, or do you have an AA meeting?"

Rita shook her head. "Not tonight. I need a few minutes to get ready, though." She glanced at the clock behind Sarah. "Whose truck was that?"

Sarah bustled to the bath, her step lightened by the farmer's kindness. "Floyd Shackles. He brought me sheep."

"He what?" Rita cast a quizzical glance up the stairs.

"Never mind." Laughing, Sarah hurried the rest of the way. "I'll explain in the car."

* * *

"Amazing." Rita pressed her point as they headed home following the evening service. "How they used the Good Shepherd story right after that farmer brought you the sheep."

"Saint John used sheep and lamb analogies often," observed Sarah. "It's not that unusual."

"But laying down your life for your sheep," Rita continued. "Sarah, that was almost you."

"*Almost* being the operative word." Sarah kept her tone light with effort. She, too, had been touched by the focus of the prayer service. "It was nice to have Rev. Weilers there with Pastor Zigarowicz."

"Doing it together brings a nice crowd," Rita noted. "Craig was there."

"Oh?"

"In the back. On the other side."

"I didn't see him."

"He made sure you didn't." Rita turned, facing her sister-in-law. "He ducked out as the pastors offered the blessing."

"Oh."

"Yeah. Oh." Rita sent her a look she only half caught as she concentrated on driving. "Most guys would have given up by now, Sarah."

"He's a slow learner."

"Or especially vested." Rita gave her arm a little poke. "Name me two things wrong with the guy."

"He's cocky and hates Slocums in general."

"I'd say self-assured and handles certain Slocums with an understandable air of diffidence," Rita corrected her. "Others he finds singularly attractive."

"A new turn of events," Sarah retorted, her newfound peace evaporating. "Reet, look at me. My face is a mess. A train wreck, minimal. I have no idea what the outcome of all this will be, but I know one thing. Craig Macklin likes beauty. It's in everything he does. His home, his family, the sweep of his yard, his old girlfriends. He's a man who appreciates God-given splendor and I'm fresh out. Not like I had all that much to begin with," she finished with a self-deprecating scowl.

"You're nuts," Rita shot back. "Yeah, you've hit a rough road right now, but you're beautiful, Sarah. A man looks at you and sees the forces of nature come together, that's how lovely you are. Don't you see that?"

"I see a woman of mixed blood who never truly belonged in the realm of man, but does well in a field of sheep," Sarah replied.

Rita smiled. "Marriage to a sheep will never be sanctioned in the church."

"Not everyone is meant for marriage," Sarah told her. "I'm content with my home. My family. Some of them, at least." She offered Rita a little smile. "I want to be grateful for what I have, Reet. Not hunger for what's out of my reach."

"But what if it's not out of reach?" Rita pressed. She faced Sarah more fully. "What if your stubbornness blocks you from discerning God's plan?"

Sarah remembered the morning's reflection in the upstairs mirror. "I'm hideous, Rita."

"Sarah—"

"What's this?" Turning into the driveway, Sarah noted Brett, Liv and Skeeter at the barn entrance. "Is everything okay?" she called. She shoved Rita's car into park and pushed open her door, then hurried to the waiting children.

"More sheep, Aunt Sarah," crowed Skeeter, rubbing her fingers through the wool of the ewe behind her. "People dropped them off while you were gone."

"God love them," breathed Rita, reaching in to stroke the new arrivals. "How many?"

"Six more," said Brett. "I isolated the others so we won't spread anything. What do you think, Aunt Sarah? Pretty nice?"

"Very nice," she confirmed, stepping into the confined area where Brett had the new arrivals. "And you did just the right thing, Brett. Who brought them?"

Brett named three local farmers and their wives. "They were

sorry to miss you," he told her sincerely. "They all wished you well tomorrow."

Tomorrow. Somehow these people knew her surgery loomed and were doing their best to raise her spirits. Strengthen her.

You shouldn't go into surgery all riled up like this. Craig's voice came back to haunt her.

Had he done this? Arranged this? Even just encouraged it, hoping for her peace of mind before surgery?

Her heart spun at the thought. Could he have pulled this off, then sat there in church, praying for her?

Oh, yeah. He was plenty capable of it, that's for sure. But, why? Why on earth would he bother?

Only one answer came to mind and it wasn't one she found easy to believe, but she went to bed that night hoping and praying the facial surgeon could work magic. Despite her words in the car, Sarah wanted to emerge from her surgical chrysalis a butterfly, strong and lovely.

She'd had more than enough of being the worm.

Chapter Twenty-One

"More coffee?" Craig asked, nodding to Rita's foam cup the next morning.

She jerked, glanced at the cup as though just aware of it, then brought her gaze to his. "I didn't drink this one." Rueful, she rose and dumped the cold contents into the waiting room sink, then trashed the cup. "I'm a tea drinker, actually. How long has it been?"

"Nearly an hour."

"The surgeon said it wouldn't take long," Rita reminded him. "Fairly simple. Those were her words."

"Better she takes her time," Craig consoled. "Gets it right. Sarah's pretty sensitive about the whole thing."

"You got that right." Rita's tone left no room for dispute. Concerned, she eyed the arch separating the surgical unit. "I hope this works. Sarah's never been assured about her looks. To have this happen…" Her voice faded. She clasped her hands, fingers straining.

Craig eyed her, surprised. "Sarah's one of the most self-assured women I've ever met."

"It seems like that, doesn't it?" Rita noted. "And she is, in many ways. She relies on her faith to see her through. But her looks? Her appearance?" Rita shook her head, her expression grave. "She's always had a rough self-image. She just hides it well."

"But she's beautiful." Craig's assertion left no room for discussion. He pictured Sarah's face, the warmth of her features. The perfect blend of cultures that gave her honeyed skin, soulful eyes, the black wave of hair that reached mid-back in a braid. How often had he wondered what it would be like to run his hands through that hair. "How could she not know how lovely she is?"

Rita snorted, disgusted. "You can't figure it out?"

Marc's words came back to him. His hands clenched, imagining what Sarah's life had been like with Tom Jr. and Ed. The years without her mother's protection. Sarah may not have been physically harmed by her older half siblings, but emotional abuse? Mental anguish? The probability became crystal clear. Tom and Ed were clever enough to cause long-term suffering. His grandparents were living proof of that. Why hadn't he realized the seriousness of their effect on Sarah?

Sarah'd run as far as she could. You couldn't get much farther than New Zealand. She'd come back mature, ready to forge a life of her own, but ended up in the North Country because Rita needed her. The kids needed her.

And now he needed her.

Craig clenched his jaw. No wonder she erected instant battlements after the accident. If she'd been uncertain of her attractiveness before, the current reflection must seem horrific. He shook his head. "I had no idea," he confessed to Rita. She frowned, puzzled. "Her thoughts. Her fears. I mean, I see banged-up victims all the time."

"Comparing Sarah to one of your four-footed friends might not get you far," Rita cautioned, smiling.

Craig smiled back. "Good point. No, I mean the disfigurement. I see it from a doctor's viewpoint, another thing to fix." He lifted his shoulders, nonchalant. "No big deal. We observe, assess and delegate." He shook his head, his fingers clasped. "I never thought of it from Sarah's mind-set."

"Sarah keeps her emotions private."

"But I should have realized," Craig argued, standing. He paced the room. "I looked at the physical and ignored the psychological."

"Oh, your little sheep campaign was a positive touch," Rita offered with a smile.

"Sheep campaign?"

"The farmers who came last night, donating sheep. Eight, in all. All pregnant ewes. To help Sarah rebuild her flock. You encouraged them, right?"

Craig shook his head. "I have no idea what you're talking about. I didn't—" With a start, he stopped mid-sentence. "I was ordering new rotational fencing for her at Tractor Supply," he recalled out loud. "One of the farmers asked how many sheep were lost and I told them." He frowned, remembering. "Floyd Shackles was saying what a shame it was, that she was such a good example and all. I agreed. Mentioned her upcoming surgery. Then they loaded the fencing and I brought it home. Figured I'd install the fence today, while she's here. The farmers must have worked it out amongst themselves." He shot Rita a half smile. "They admire her."

"Me, too," Rita agreed. "She stood by me all along. Who knows where I'd be now, where my kids would be, if it weren't for Sarah White Fawn."

"White Fawn?"

"Her middle name," Rita explained. "Peg wanted both heritages reflected in her name. As the story goes, Old Tom was too drunk to care, so Sarah was christened Sarah White Fawn Slocum. Since Sarah means 'Princess', it translates to 'Princess White Fawn.'"

"That's beautiful."

"And it suits. But her mother taught her that names change with life stages. You can grow out of one name and into another. Her hope was for Sarah to grow into her grandmother's name. Wise Woman."

"I'd say she got her wish."

"Me, too. But our little Wise Woman got knocked for a

loop in that storm. Lately she's been more like Wise-mouth Woman. Snippy."

Craig didn't argue that point. Inspired by their conversation, he withdrew his cell phone. "I've got to make a quick call. Grab me if you hear anything."

Rita nodded. "I promise."

Outside, Craig dialed Brooks' wood shop. The woodman answered on the third ring. "Woodcrafter."

"Brooks?"

"That you, Doc?"

"Yeah. I've got two things to get straight with you. It's a definite yes on the Adirondack bed. The log one. King-sized. Let's go with a medium-toned stain. Not too dark, but not too light, either."

"Fruitwood might be nice," Brooks offered, his voice mulling. "Or a honey tone. Maybe pecan."

"Can you do up a sample?"

"I'll have it ready this afternoon," Brooks promised. "If you're ready, you can pick out dressers to match and I'll blend enough stain for everything."

"Good."

"And the second thing?" Brooks' voice held a note of interest.

"I need Hy Everts to carve me a deer. A fawn. A white fawn. Maybe even a doe and fawn together." Hy's intricate carvings were marketed online and through Brooks' store. His work was well respected. A widower, the older man gave glory to God and nature by re-creating it in various types of wood.

"A white fawn, you say?" Brooks' voice went thoughtful. "Like the ones on that old army base?" The Seneca Army depot had become home to a full herd of rare white deer. Because of the base's fenced-in structure, the recessive gene reproduced itself in unusually large numbers. What was rare in the wild became commonplace there, drawing tourists in hopes of photo ops.

"Exactly."

"You need it quick?"

"Naw." Craig knew better than to rush an artisan. "Tell him to take his time. Any pose he wants."

"I'm on it," Brooks replied, the pencil scratch audible. "Anything else?"

"No. I'll stop by this afternoon and check out those color samples."

"How's our shepherd doing? Still in surgery?"

Craig hadn't mentioned where he was, but not much got by Brooks. "Yes. No news yet."

"I'm praying for her."

In all Craig's years he'd never seen Brooks Harriman enter a church, yet a more spiritual man he'd never met. "Thanks, Brooks. That means a lot. I better get back upstairs."

"You do that. I'll catch you later."

Disconnecting the call, Craig mulled Brooks' words.

Obviously the woodcrafter had a pretty good handle on Craig's personal life. Hadn't he cautioned Craig about the differences between hardwood and veneer?

And here Craig was, wanting hardwood all the way. Go figure.

The scent of flowers stirred Sarah's senses. She glimpsed her mother running, laughing as she gathered wildflowers. "We'll dry them with baby's breath," she called over her shoulder. "Make pretty bouquets for winter."

"Like in Sarah, Plain and Tall?" little Sarah asked, chasing her mother's flowing skirt.

"Exactly like that." Turning, the older woman caught Sarah in a hug, spinning her through the meadow. "Only there is nothing plain about this Sarah. She's beauty, through and through."

"Really?"

"Really, truly. I would never lie to you, Sarah White Fawn. A mother always tells the truth."

"Hey. You're waking up. How we doing, Princess?"

"I smell flowers." Confused, Sarah scanned the room, searching. "Is Mama here?"

Craig leaned down. "Afraid not, honey. Just Rita and me. And flowers. You must have been dreaming."

His voice sent warmth cruising through her. The tenderness in his tone was not unlike her mother's, but his eyes reflected a different kind of caring. She swallowed hard, then brought a hand to her cheek. "How did it go?"

"Very well." The surgeon moved into Sarah's viewing range and beamed. "There'll be some understandable swelling and bruising, but there was no apparent nerve damage or serious fragmentation. We're clear. You may—" she pointed out, nodding to Sarah's face "—experience some numbness from swollen tissues pressing on the nerve, but that should dissipate as the healing progresses."

Sarah hated to ask this question with Craig around, but she needed to know. "How will I look when it's done?" She felt Craig's eyes on her, but kept her attention turned to the doctor.

"Beautiful," he interjected.

Sarah ignored him. The doctor's lips twitched in sympathy. "He's right. I anticipate no lasting damage. You should heal well and we've hidden the surgical scars. You can feel some stitches inside your mouth." Watching Sarah probe her cheek with her tongue, the doctor nodded. "The other cuts are at the hairline of the temple and the lower edge of your eyebrow. They shouldn't be discernible once healed."

Craig pressed a kiss to her forehead. His tenderness coupled with the doctor's assurance had hot tears stinging her eyes. "You're sure?"

The surgeon didn't waver. "It's my job, Sarah. I do it well. I'll stop by later to check on you."

"Thank you." Sarah clasped the doctor's hand. "Thank you so much."

"You're welcome." Nodding to Rita and Craig, the doctor left, her footsteps firm against the speckled tile floors.

"I want a mirror."

"Remember what the doctor said," Rita warned. "Bruising

and swelling are normal. There's a six-week recovery from this."

"That bad, huh?" Seeing Rita's discomfort, Sarah shifted her eyes to Craig. "I'm hideous."

"Nope."

"Freak of nature."

"Sarah—"

"Circus material."

"Stop it." His voice showed little patience with this line of thought. "Surgery leaves reminders. That's normal. At least you're not a dog. She didn't have to shave your face, denude your jowls."

"Your bedside manner could use practice."

The look on his face said he agreed. She ignored it, thrusting out a hand. With a flick of her wrist, she opened the hinged personal compartment on her service tray. The mirror sprang into view. Her color drained at the first look.

Craig reached to flip it down. Her hand impeded his. "Don't."

The reflection was no better than when she'd checked in hours before. Worse, actually. She had no idea where the lump of bitter disappointment sprang from. She'd known what to expect, the healing entailed post-surgery, but somehow, she'd prepared herself for some kind of improvement. Some vestige of repair.

Hadn't happened. Biting her lip, she flipped the tray top down with a thump and slid beneath the covers. "Please go."

"Sarah." Craig leaned forward, his hand stroking her forehead. "Give it time. Please."

"Just go." Her voice wavered, precarious.

Rita touched his arm. Her look of sympathy was accompanied by a nod to the door. He understood and agreed, but didn't like it. Still, upsetting Sarah with his presence wasn't the best idea. He straightened. "I should get to work. I'll see you soon."

"No."

He drew a breath, ready to argue, then stopped, common sense pushing him to walk away, allow her time.

How could he? She needed him, despite what she thought. No way could he turn his back on her now. She needed his comfort, his reassurance.

Craig's stomach churned. The look of anguish marring Sarah's bandaged features urged him to soothe. How could he reject that silent summons?

"For the Lord comforts his people and will have compassion on his afflicted ones." The words from Isaiah pressed upon his heart. He needed to trust in God's strength, His love for Sarah a constant, ever-present.

To leave Sarah broken and bandaged, hurt and hostile, went against his grain. He was a doctor, trained to heal. He'd spent no small number of sleepless nights treating sick and injured pets and livestock. How could a man dedicated to saving all creatures, great and small, turn from the woman who'd won his heart?

Craig swallowed hard.

Maybe this was a hurdle he couldn't scale with Sarah, much as he'd like to. Maybe it was a battle she had to forge alone. Not alone, he corrected himself. God was with her, holding her. Cherishing her, even after Craig had yelled at Him in indignation. He stepped back and nodded. "All right, then. When you're feeling better, let me know. Or come visit. You know where I live. Well." He gave Sarah a rueful nod. "Almost live."

Rita sent him an encouraging smile. "You should be able to move out of the camper soon, right?"

"Late summer," Craig replied, "depending on how things go." Fighting his desire to stay, Craig squeezed Sarah's hand. "Patience, Wise Woman."

Her chin quivered. Her lips trembled. His throat tightened in response. He stepped away, choking down emotion. "I'll be around."

Rita nodded, her expression sympathetic.

Sarah didn't say a word.

* * *

Craig's phone paged him as he finished the last side of Sarah's new fencing. Seeing his mother's number, he returned the call quickly. If it wasn't vital, she left a voice mail. Important, she paged. He heard it in her voice when she answered.

"Mom?"

"Craig." Silence filled the gap while she caught her breath. Struggled against tears.

"Mom, what is it?" Setting the last rod into place, he swung the wire gate to make the final connection. "What's wrong?"

"It's Rocket."

His heart sank. He didn't have to ask. The truth colored her voice, her tears.

"I found him under the back deck. I called Dad, but there was nothing we could do. It looks like he just fell asleep and…"

Craig understood *and*. He blew out a breath, fighting the pressure in his chest. "I'm on my way."

He passed landmarks without seeing them. By the time he made his way up the lodge drive, he had no idea how he'd gotten home. Thoughts of Rocket filled his head. The boy and hound, bounding through fields, neither one a hunter, despite their heritage.

Oh, it had been interesting, all right, to be Jim Macklin's son and Cade's brother and never want to aim a gun. With their top-notch reputations, Craig had learned the skills of a gunman, then chose not to use them. When one spent his life repairing animals, it seemed at odds to hunt them down.

Since Rocket bombed as a bird dog, they made a good pair. Never once had his father lamented the lack of hunting prowess in young man or beast. In typical fashion, he'd let them mature as they were destined.

Now Rocket had passed. Funny. Craig would have sworn he was prepared for this moment, but he was wrong. The sight of the shrouded hound brought him to his knees, tears unchecked as he petted the smooth head of his beloved friend, the thick paws stilled forevermore, the dog's warm, faithful heart silenced.

Cade showed up soon after. Together they hoisted Rocket in his burial sling, moving him to a gravesite slightly uphill.

"He liked to sit here," Deb explained, waving a hand, Jim's arm snug around her shoulders. "In the afternoons, he would watch for your car. See you coming. Remember how he used to run down and greet you, Craig?"

Craig nodded, swiping the back of his hand across his face. "Yeah."

"Of course these days he'd just thump his tail. Wait for you to come to him," she continued, her voice breaking. How many women would have unconditional love for a gassy bird dog that refused to fetch a bird? "He was a good old man."

"He was," Grams agreed, a sweater pulled tight despite the warm afternoon. "Your grandpa used to say that a true dog was a true friend, and Rocket was all that." She bent and stroked the old dog's head. "Sleep well, my friend."

Craig's throat thickened. His vision blurred.

With gentle hands they lowered Rocket into his final resting spot. Once the task was complete and the hole filled, Craig grasped the hands of those on either side of him, not caring that some might think it weird to eulogize a dog. Rocket was more than a dog. He was a buddy, a confidant. A friend in need. "Father, we thank You for the gift of Rocket. His faithfulness. His patience. His unqualified devotion. You sent him to us in spite of his flaws and we'll miss him."

Grams squeezed his hand. A chorus of "Amens" sounded around them. Craig turned. A small group of fishermen had gathered. One of the men blessed himself, his eyes moist. Craig nodded in understanding.

"Stay for supper, Craig?"

His mother's voice held a plea, but Craig couldn't face that. He didn't want food or casual conversation. He wanted two things he couldn't have—his dog by his side, jumping logs and scaring fish, and Sarah Slocum's love.

Neither scenario seemed possible. One was dead, the other despairing.

Driving home, he alternated between laments. The dog, whose life had been strong and fulfilling, ending in a peaceful, natural death, and Sarah, whose misconceptions made her a repository of self-doubt.

"I don't know how to help her, God," he prayed as he passed her tree-shrouded home, the windows dark. "How do I reassure her when I was part of the problem? I saw her as a Slocum, not thinking of her feelings, her emotions. How do I make up for that?"

Once home, he pushed out of the driver's seat and walked to the back of the house. From this vantage point, the land opened before him, its beauty resplendent. Rolling fields melded into forestland, with occasional houses and farms dotting the landscape. The North Country bore all kinds of people, from all walks of life. His view encompassed that. A feeling of entirety lay before him.

But he preferred the view from the front of his house. Sarah's pasture, her front hay lot. The barn with its noises and smells. The small corner of the house visible between the trees. The light that shined through the branches at night, offering a glimmer of hope.

"Give her peace, Lord. Help her see what I see. The woman of beauty and promise. Help her find the truth no matter what the surgery leaves."

Sleep was hard-found that night, and restless once it came. Disjointed images of Sarah and Rocket filled his brain. He awoke more tired than when he'd lain down, and took a bracing, cold shower to clear his head.

Then went to work like it was any old day.

Chapter Twenty-Two

"Walk over and thank him."

Rita sounded irked. Sarah bit back a retort, thinking of Rita's steady improvement. Two months ago she'd have been drunk and passed out, not reprimanding Sarah's lack of manners.

"I'll send a card." Sarah tried to nudge the tired note from her voice. She'd slept upright since the surgery, and not all that well. Each day she watched for signs of improvement. Nothing so far. Until there was, facing Craig didn't make the short list.

"Will you stop looking at your face already?"

Sarah drew back from the mirror, bemused.

"It needs time to heal," her sister-in-law continued. "And you need to march across the street and thank Craig Macklin for that fencing."

"He shouldn't have done it." Sarah hoped her manner left little room for response.

Wrong.

"But he did and you're acting like a brat."

"Rita June." Sarah sent her sister-in-law a look of surprise. "You just called me a name."

"And meant it."

"Naw. You didn't." Smiling, Sarah settled back to her balance sheets. To allow healing time, Brett had taken over

Sarah's farm duties before working for Craig at night. The Bristols filled in where necessary, leaving Sarah time to rest her bones while working on accounts. Spreadsheets were gravy work, even with pain pills coursing through her system.

Brett pushed through the back door, his footsteps heavy. "Hey. Can I have some of that butter cake to take to Craig's?"

"Of course." Rita stood and moved to the counter. "Take as much as you'd like. You've been working hard."

"It's not that," Brett replied. He watched as she sliced off a generous hunk. "His dog died the other day and he seems really sad about it."

"Rocket?" Sarah rose quickly. "Rocket died?"

"Yeah. The day you had your surgery."

The day she tossed him from her hospital room. Great. Just great. Talk about kicking a man when he's down. Of course the dog must have died later. She'd have known if Craig had gone through that, wouldn't she? The look of him? His actions?

No, she admitted. She'd been too caught up in herself to pay attention to Craig. She couldn't rightfully say what expression he'd worn that day, she'd cut him down so swiftly.

"How's he doing?"

Brett shrugged. "Okay. Just misses him, I guess. Said it was weird because he hadn't been able to do much with him for over a year, but it still seems funny to have him gone."

"I bet." Making a decision, she eyed her nephew. "How late are you working?"

"Not late. Craig's got tomorrow off and we need to let the wallboard seams dry."

Craig would be home tomorrow. Good.

"Did you want me to tell him something?"

She shook her head. "No. I..." She fingered the hem of her cotton shirt, thinking. "I hope he enjoys the cake."

Brett frowned. Rita eyed her with a little more frankness as she resumed her seat in front of the monitor. Once Brett left, Rita spoke up. "What are you planning?"

"That you might be right. Maybe it's time I stop dwelling on Sarah, the freak."

Rita groaned. Sarah smiled with care. Until the bone healed, there wasn't much incentive to grin. The accompanying pain made it less than worthwhile. But God had dropped an opportunity into her lap.

She hated indebtedness. Her self-reliance cringed at the thought of owing anyone.

That made it hard to accept the sheep, but they were from other farmers, like herself. People unafraid to get dirty.

Craig's gifts were different. Crippling, almost. She might start depending on his help and generosity, and then where would she be? Waiting for the broken heart to follow. As sorry as she was about the death of his dog, she was ready to seize the opportunity.

She only wished she looked better. A glance to the mirror confirmed her fears and had Rita threatening its demise. "I'll break it. The surgeon said six weeks, minimum."

"It's a long time to look like this, Rita."

Rita swung around. "The storm could have killed you. It did kill sixteen full-grown sheep and their lambs. You might want to thank God for sparing you instead of belly-aching. Whining is even more unbecoming than bruising."

Rita was right. She knew it. But the mirror's pull was strong, its reflective image reaffirming every negative thing she'd tried to leave behind. "I'm tired."

Grim, Rita nodded. "I've got things covered here. Maybe you should rest."

Agreeing, Sarah saved her work, shut down the program and climbed the stairs. As she crested the top, Rita's voice carried after her. "And stay away from the mirrors."

Sarah paused, surveying the lovely home before her, a box clutched in her hands. The house rose from the land but seemed part of it, its style and grace suited to the hillside setting. Turning, she saw her holdings as Craig must see them, worn and small, cluttered with animals, farm equipment and dung. Self-conscious, she took a step in retreat, ready to flee.

A small sound came from the box. Hearing it, she stiffened her spine, thrust her chin up and pretended her face was whole. With a firm hand, she knocked on Craig's front door.

No answer.

She tried again.

Still no answer. Frowning, she eyed the SUV. If his car was here, then by rights—

With a blast of realization, she wondered if he'd gone out last night. Hadn't Brett said they weren't working late?

He probably had a date and sent the kid home early. *Stupid, Sarah. Just plain stupid.*

She started down the walk, chin dipped, her footsteps hurried. Why hadn't she considered he might have gone out with someone else? How awkward. Heat flamed her cheeks as she headed home.

"Sarah?"

Craig's deep tone stopped her. She turned, wondering what she was doing there, nonplussed by the sound of his voice. She drew a breath and looked up.

He strode toward her from the back of the house, his expression curious, a tool belt snug around his hips. Really nice hips that looked good in worn blue jeans. The thinning side seams made the denims either very expensive or well-worn. Knowing Craig like she did now, Sarah put her money on well-worn and oft-washed. "You came over."

"I..." Glancing around, she clamped her lips, willing her nerves to calm. "Yes."

"To see the house?" His voice was gentle. Hopeful. He leaned forward, head angled.

"No. Brett told me about Rocket."

Craig's eyes shadowed. "Not the greatest week."

"I wanted to tell you how sorry I was," Sarah explained. "I know what he meant to you." She hesitated, looking beyond him. "It's hard to say goodbye, even when you know it's time."

"Yes." He stood before her, those jeans resting on narrow hips, his shoulders straining the seams of an aged v-neck white T. He watched her, then offered, "I thought I was ready. Was sure of it. When the time came?" He shook his head, grimacing. "Not even close."

She nodded and moved closer. "It was like that with my mother. I understood the disease, knew the inevitability and even prayed for a peaceful death when the pain grew bad, but…" She shrugged again. "I still wasn't ready."

"I don't think anyone's ever ready to lose their mother," Craig replied, motioning her to the front step. She moved forward and sat, positioning the box on her lap. "As much as I loved Rocket, you've got me beat."

She smiled at his gentle humor. The warmth in his tone. The way he stood by her, then sat as if sheltering her. He nudged her hip with his. "I'm glad you came by. I've been hoping you would."

"Because?"

"Because I miss you and want to show you my house. See what Brett and I have been working on."

"When you're not busy replacing your neighbor's fencing," she retorted.

He shifted a brow up. "Am I in trouble?"

Sarah eyed the trees, the chirps and whistles of mid-summer birdsong a sound of contentment. Joy. Listening, she almost forgot what she looked like. How she appeared. Then her cheek sent a twinge into her temple and reality flooded back.

Quickly she turned her head, softening his view.

"Sarah."

She ignored the gentle remonstration. "I brought you something."

His hand grazed the sweep of her good cheek. She fought the sensation his touch aroused while he smiled. "Did you? I loved the butter cake."

"Rita," she replied, keeping her bad side turned away. "My gift is different."

"Brownies?"

She almost laughed. "No. This." Handing him the box, she watched as he lifted the lid.

"Sarah. It's—"

"Little Lady," she supplied, smiling. "She loves you and misses you, so I thought—"

He might never know what she thought. His mouth closed over hers, the kiss gentle but full, the feel of him, strength and muscle, soft mouth and firm hands a glorious contradiction. The whimper of the pup pulled them apart long moments later.

"Craig, I didn't—"

"Mean for that to happen?" His smile deepened. He pressed a kiss to the undamaged side of her forehead. "I did. Been waiting for quite some time and wouldn't mind having it happen again, truth be told. Often. Regularly."

"I wanted you to have the dog. She was taken with you and I thought you'd be lonely without Rocket." She stood and faced him square. He pushed off the step, smiling, the box with the pup braced in one hand.

"You were right. I'm very lonely." His eyes sparkled with something that had nothing to do with dogs. His hand strayed to her good cheek, her neck, sending wishes and dreams spiraling through her. She took a broad step back.

"I didn't do this as a come on. Or to flirt with you. I just wanted to repay kindness with kindness."

"A trade-off?"

His tone made her blink. "Kind of."

"Because I replaced the fencing."

"I don't like being indebted," she explained, wishing she had better words. "It makes me uncomfortable."

"I see."

He studied her, head angled, eyes narrowed. "So I get the pick of the litter as long as it doesn't include you?"

Her face flooded with embarrassment. "I'm not a dog to be picked over by potential buyers."

"Nor a woman to be loved and cherished?"

"Like your last one?"

She didn't mean to say it. She saw the effect of her accusation like a dash of cold water against his face. Then his features went cool and calm. Carefully blank. "Well. It's good to know where we stand." He stepped back, holding the box with strong, gentle hands. Setting it down, he withdrew the pup and nuzzled her neck. "I guess we're even, Miss Slocum."

Sarah's heart pinched. Short minutes ago he'd laid his lips on hers, giving her a hint of what could be with a man like Craig Macklin. A quick taste of the love she'd never dared hope for.

But like her father and brothers, it was withdrawn with haste and rightly so. Everyone knew a Macklin couldn't abide a Slocum.

The memory of his kiss lingered. The touch of his mouth. She brought her hand to her lips to hold the pleasure, but it had already fled. He watched her, his face unmoving, inscrutable.

Solemn, silent, she turned and walked away.

Chapter Twenty-Three

"A soccer ball at work?" Rita smiled as her gaze swept the ball in Brett's hands. "Nice job, kid."

"Craig lets me shoot on him for practice," Brett explained. "I want to try out for the modified team next week."

"But you haven't played in…" Sarah's stomach clenched as the timeline reflected itself in Rita's expression. "Over two years."

"That's why I need to practice," Brett countered, watching her, his tone cautious. He and Liv stepped carefully around Rita, not ready to be themselves. It was a phony level of safety, but Sarah could do little except watch and wait. Eventually someone would act normal, and Rita would either withstand her first crisis or not.

Sarah prayed for the former.

"When are tryouts?" Sarah asked.

Brett swung his gaze to hers. "Monday morning. Craig said he'd drop me off if someone else could pick me up."

"Of course." Rita nodded agreement, but her expression was guarded. "Being out of practice, it'll be a rough go, Brett."

"I know." He nodded, stoic. "But I want to try."

"Then you should."

He swung out the door, a hand in the air. "See you later."

"He'll never make it."

Sarah and Rita turned together. Liv stood framed in the arch between the living room and downstairs bedroom. She frowned, concerned. "Those other kids have played on travel teams while Brett's been watching TV. There's no way he can match their skill level."

"He was always good," Rita reminded them, her voice taut.

"Not good enough to overcome two years not playing," Liv contended. "I wondered why he started running last week. Must be trying to get into shape."

"Is he?" Rita looked surprised that she hadn't noticed.

"He goes early, before his barn work."

Sarah slipped in a change of subject. "Liv, can you get that side garden weeded for me? I can't do hands and knees work yet."

Liv didn't look thrilled, but she nodded. "Yeah. I'll do it now, before Shannon comes by. We're going back-to-school shopping."

Rita's look of concern heightened. "Shop small. There's not much in the budget."

Liv bit her lip and headed toward the door. "I've got what I saved from Aunt Sarah. It's a start."

Rita met Sarah's look. "You're paying her?"

"Here and there. Some for babysitting. Some for yard work. Housework was a given."

"I can't do that for them at home," Rita scolded, her ire cranked a notch.

"They know that. I told Liv she could still work for me once school's started. Weekends, anyway. And the Cromwells want her to babysit the twins from time to time."

"They do?" Rita fingered the buttons on her shirt, her expression wary. "Even with my problems?"

"You're working to overcome your problems," Sarah reminded her. "And doing well. Don't borrow trouble, Reet."

"I don't have to. Brett is setting himself up for major disappointment and Liv is about to realize our accumulated funds will buy her a sweater. Maybe two. I just hate disappointing them all the time."

"You don't," Sarah comforted. "Things are hard right now."

"Because their father was a thief and I'm weak," Rita retorted.

"Sooooo...my turn's over?"

"Excuse me?"

Sarah blinked, long and slow. "My turn to whine? Feel sorry for myself? It must have officially ended because you've taken the reins."

Rita flushed.

Sarah grinned. "No, really, keep going. You've been tough for weeks now. Give it your best shot."

Rita looked torn between laughter and tears. Humor won. As she giggled, Sarah crossed the room and hugged her, laughing along with her. "What a pair," she teased, hugging Rita's arm. "Let's get out of here. Go for a walk. I'm tired of walls, tired of shade. I want to feel the sun on my face. The wind in my hair. Eat really good ice cream."

"How cliché."

Sarah grinned as she slipped into scuffed-up sneakers. "But true."

Spying the two women, Craig released the caulk gun trigger.

Sarah looked better. He couldn't see her face from this distance, but her walk looked lighter.

He'd prayed for that, wanting her peace of mind, knowing she needed to come to terms with her past. Deal with it, somehow. An angst he hadn't known existed until the accident brought it to the foreground.

She'd hidden it behind the placid look, the calm demeanor. But Rita was right. There were serious self-confidence issues Sarah needed to wrestle with before she'd ever give her heart fully.

When she did, he had every intention of being on the receiving end.

The women looked up and saw him, perched on his roof-clearing ladder. He raised his arm in a friendly wave. The ladder shifted north. He leaned left to compensate, forcing it to sway back. Once it stilled, he turned back.

Rita waved.

Sarah stopped dead, a hand to her mouth as the ladder shifted again. Seeing that, he rocked it once more for effect, watching her reaction. Even from this distance, he saw her eyes widen. Her mouth open. He turned away, grinning.

Naw. She wasn't interested at all. Not a bit.

Right.

"You don't use that dangerous ladder at Craig's, do you, Brett?"

Scooping ice cream into a cone, Brett paused. "What dangerous ladder?"

"The aluminum one that reaches beyond the front roof. I don't want you on it," Sarah insisted. "It's faulty."

"Why do you think that?"

"Because she saw Craig swaying on it tonight and she's convinced it's the path to an early grave," remarked his mother as she fluted edges of a pie.

"Oh. That." Brett licked his ice cream, nonchalant. "He does that all the time."

"What?" Sarah stared at him, her mind racing.

"Moves the ladder. He can actually walk it along the ground if he wants to."

"While he's on it?" Sarah's voice pitched up.

"If the ground's hard enough," Brett added, admiration edging his tone. "It's cool. Kind of like stilts."

Like stilts. Right. Only twice as high and way more dangerous. Sarah ignored the look Rita sent her. Smacking her hand against the counter, she shrugged into a lightweight hoodie, ignoring Brett's confusion. "I'm checking the back pasture."

"I did that already."

She waved a hand and pretended not to hear Rita's snicker as she trudged away.

Right then Sarah was pretty sure if Craig Macklin toppled from his show-off ladder into an early grave she'd have no regrets. She wouldn't even take the time to attend the funeral, not with so much work and all.

So why did her heart jump when she saw the ladder sway? Why did she have to fight the urge to run and save the big clown?

Because she couldn't imagine a life without him any more than she could envision a life with him. She, who never straddled an issue, was trapped in the middle of this one. The mirror appeared kinder today, much to her relief. A vestige of her former appearance came through. Though she didn't appreciate it before, she was pleased to welcome its return. Funny, she'd always thought her looks a challenge until they really were. Her appreciation of her natural attributes was growing as healing progressed.

The smell hit Sarah as she walked through the kitchen door a few nights later. Pungent. Sour. There was no mistaking it, not anymore. Filled with dread, she approached the stairs. "Rita?"

Nothing.

She mounted the steps quietly. "Rita? You up here?" Peeking in various doors, she found sleeping children, but no Rita. Hurrying back downstairs, the smell grew stronger. She called again. "Rita? Where are you?"

"Here."

Rita sat in the far corner of the darkened front bedroom, a bottle by her side. It was open, but full. Almost.

"What's happened?"

Rita stared outside. "What hasn't?"

Sarah waited, uncertain. "Are we playing twenty questions? Give me a hint, huh?" Cautious, she edged into the room and perched on the corner of the bed.

"You don't need a hint. I'll spell it out for you. Brett didn't make the team because his mother's been too drunk to get him to games and practice, Liv can't afford the pants to go with the sweaters she bought because surprise, surprise, there isn't enough money, and I just got my second quarter statement from Tom's cooperative retirement fund, showing a net worth of over one hundred and thirty thousand dollars in his account." Flicking her wrist, Rita sent the funds statement flying through the air. "And I can't buy my kid a pair of decent blue jeans."

Sarah caught the paper statement. Jaw tight, she had no idea what to say. How to comfort. "Rita, I—"

"There's nothing you can say," Rita interrupted. "I can't give Brett back the two years I wasted. Years that might have cost him any chance he had of playing on the high school team next year. Liv's spent that same time raising her brother and sister because I was too drunk to do a proper job of it. Skeeter?" Rita mulled the glass of whiskey she held to her face, inhaling deeply. "She'll have plenty to tell Oprah, won't she?"

"Have you taken a drink?" Sarah struggled to sound calm, eyeing the bottle and the glass.

"Not yet."

"Going to?"

"I'm sorely tempted." Rita gazed through the honey-toned liquid, swirling it through the bed of ice. "It smells real good."

"How can I help?" Sarah leaned forward, hands pressed to her knees. "Can I call someone? Do something?"

"No. No, Sarah." Standing, Rita gripped the glass. Sarah was afraid the tumbler would crack under the pressure, but it held. "You've done all you could, Wise Woman. Now it's between me and the bottle."

"And God."

"He doesn't drink."

"Good example, then. Hang onto Him, Rita. That faith I've always seen in you. The faith that helped you respect others when my brother cheated them. Maligned them."

Rita's face twisted into a mix of anger and shame. "I hate what he did to us. To me. Sarah, I hate the man and he fathered my three children. I look at them, and I see Tom. I hear them and I hear Tom. When they do something wrong or selfish, I see Tom and I can't forgive his crimes. How can I help them through this when I can't find a way myself?"

"News flash," Sarah told her. "They've gotten through it. Yeah, they've got some damage. But they've bounced back farther than you."

"Because they didn't share responsibility for his choices," Rita lamented. She stared through the glass, the curve warping her features. "It's no use." The glass twisted in Rita's hand, her long fingers straining white. "I am what I am. And I don't want to face it anymore."

"Rough night, huh?"

Sarah turned, surprised. Brooks Harriman stepped into the room, his eyes trained on Rita. "How does it smell?"

Rita didn't look up. Just kept her eyes on the glass, nostrils flared to capture the scent. "Real good."

"I bet." He moved to the bed with casual demeanor, lounging on the end opposite Sarah. "So. You planning to do it?"

"Maybe." Rita eyed the glass, fascinated. "Maybe not."

"Well, let me know because I'd like to go for coffee if you don't."

"I drink tea."

"They serve that as well."

Sarah leaned over. "Brooks. How—"

He waved her off. "Sarah'd be glad to get rid of that for you, Rita, while you and I head out. What do you say?"

"I want it so bad." Rita's voice thinned. Strained. Like she wrestled the devil himself.

Brooks nodded. "I know."

Sarah angled her chin, watching him. Understanding dawned over steady ticks of the wall clock.

Rita called Brooks for help. Sarah darted a glance from him to Rita and back again. Brooks acted like he had all the time in the world while Rita weighed the biggest decision of her life, her expression tight.

"I'm a lousy mother."

Brooks lifted one shoulder, his steady gaze locked on Rita. "They're young. Time to fix things, yet."

"I've got no money."

"You've got two hands and two feet, all in working order. Get a job."

To Sarah's surprise, Rita almost smiled. "I could, you know. I'm a smart woman."

"I've never doubted it." The man's face and tone were sincere.

Rita pulled a deep breath. For a long moment she looked like she might pitch the whiskey-filled tumbler across the room. Her arm arched to do just that, then she paused. Looked it over. With a sigh she handed the whole lot to Sarah and rose, reaching a hand to Brooks. He stood and grasped the hand she offered. Head angled, he eased her forward. "Let's go get that coffee."

She didn't look back. Not at Sarah, the glass or the bottle. Dropping Brooks' hand, she headed for the door, leading the way. "I said tea."

He pretended surprise, then winked at Sarah. "Oh, that's right. Tea, then." Following her out the door, he sent Sarah a reassuring look. "We'll be fine. She paged Kim, but I'm her backup. Kim's mother had a stroke so Kim was unavailable tonight." His glance indicated the discreet pager attached to the back of his waist. "I was in the shower so it took me longer than it should have." Now his gaze shifted to the door. "I'm glad it wasn't too late."

Sarah nodded, then sat once they left, a glass in one hand, a nearly full bottle of whiskey in the other. After a deep breath she rose, dumped the contents of both down the drain, wrapped the bottle in layers of newspaper to avoid the curious eyes of the recycling crew and threw it away. Restless, she went outside.

She tried to ignore Craig's yard light, the beacon of hope it offered. With the kids in bed, the sheep at peace and Rita under momentary control, the night seemed wanting.

She didn't realize she was shaking until she tried to settle into the lawn swing. Body tremors jerked her legs against the seat's wooden edge. Restless, she stood and walked to the road's edge, eyeing her neighbor's yard. His drive.

She'd seen him twice since the ladder incident, both times in passing. He'd tipped his hat the first time, a sun-bleached Syracuse Orangemen cap that had seen its share of wear. She'd nodded back, biting her lip, tamping her pulse.

The other time had been after church. He didn't stop, or even slow down all that much. Rita had accompanied her and the kids to Holy Trinity. Pastor Weilers welcomed Rita in his typical open style. Craig's glance noted the scene, then caught her eye. He didn't wink, didn't tilt his head and give her that slow, amused smile, the one that quickened her pulse. He'd offered a quick nod, a brief meeting of the eyes. "Sarah."

She'd colored at the single word, despite her best efforts. Not that the world in general would detect it. Her bronzed skin tone was forgiving when it came to blushing, but somehow Craig always noticed.

Not that day, though, so why was she walking the roadside, willing him to come out? Talk to her. Share her burdens.

Leaning back, Sarah stared into the night. Stars twinkled and planets glowed, their steadier light mute testimony to their solidity. The moon hung, nearly full, its light dimming nearby stars.

Her ancestors had used these beacons. They'd planted and harvested, mapping seasons by the stars. Gazing upward, she felt an almost physical tug.

God. Dear God, she prayed.

Sarah curled into the top of a grassy knoll, deep in thought, listening to the voice of her heart.

She had let fear and anger consume her. It had raised its ugly, self-pitying head and gnawed at her spirit. Feelings she'd thought long buried had surged forth, their strength magnified by her lack of faith.

The grass felt cool and damp beneath her legs, the air fresh and sweet upon her face. A face that was nearly healed and no longer painful. "Beauty is fleeting, and charm deceptive," she remembered, plucking strands of grass. "How did I lose sight so quickly, Lord? It frightens me that it can happen like that. One day strong and faithful, the next cowering and timid. Is it so delicate, this balance?

"And what of these feelings I have for my neighbor?" she mused, studying the light above Craig's garage. "It would take small effort to love him as myself, but you know that. It's just… there's so much more at stake. Rita. You saw how fragile she was tonight. How can I do something that might push her over that edge? Tip the scales in disfavor?

"And Craig's grandmother? Would I be a constant reminder of the evil that took so much from her?"

The words of the 119th Psalm flooded her. "I have strayed like a lost sheep. Seek your Servant, for I have not forgotten Your commands."

But I did, she realized, leaning back, her eyes upturned. I forgot to trust, to hand over the reins. I wanted the power to reap and sow on my own, not seeking Your counsel. Your plan.

The stars hung quiet and bright above. Kitty-corner, Craig's light glowed moonlight yellow. Inside he slept, most likely, unless the pup kept him up. Warmth and contentment bathed her as she contemplated her feelings for Craig Macklin. For the moment, she'd let him sleep. Mull her choices.

Their choices.

No longer did she feel alone in this temptation. If it was of God, she'd know soon enough. If not, she'd have that answer as well.

"Strengthen me, according to Your word." How had she forgotten such an easy plea? That answer was simple. She'd let fear and pity grab hold of her heart, but no more.

Smiling, she nodded to the circle cast by Craig's yard light. "Sleep well, beloved." She grimaced at the heat the phrase infused, even with no one about to see it, then pressed cool palms to her warm cheeks, laughing at herself.

The laughter felt good. It took everything she had to hold herself back when what she really wanted to do was run to his door, throw herself into his arms and give way to the feelings accosting her.

She clamped down the urge, a hint of common sense reminding her she hadn't been all that agreeable lately. The man might find her sudden change disconcerting. Or downright crazy.

Drawing a breath, she blew him a kiss, unseen. It would do, for now.

But tomorrow...

She didn't allow herself to think his feelings might have changed with her constant rebuffs. The matter was in God's hands. What would be, would be, but Sarah mentally scanned her wardrobe, frowning. Her closet lacked clothing destined to catch a man's eye.

Shopping was a must. She eased through the door, not wanting to wake the children. She couldn't remember the last time she bought herself a new dress. Two Easters past? Maybe three?

High time, then. She slipped under the covers once she'd undressed, relieved she could lie down once more. The pillow beneath her cheek brought no pain. No suffering. Sighing, she sank into its softness.

She felt good. Happy. One with the Spirit. She dozed off, thinking of pretty frocks and a handsome man, hoping the two were compatible. A girl had to step out of barn boots once in a while.

Chapter Twenty-Four

Serious makeovers should not be undertaken alone. Sarah sought Rita's advice. "I need help."

"Admitting is the first step, Sarah." Rita looked up from the online sudoku puzzle, teasing.

Sarah scowled. "I'm serious."

"Oh, so am I," Rita returned. Then she grinned. "What's up?"

"Clothes."

"Clothes?"

"Yes."

"Are we talking particular clothes? Winter clothes? Used clothes?"

Sarah worked not to choke. "Pretty clothes."

"Pretty clothes?"

"Stop repeating what I say."

Rita grinned. "Sarah White Fawn, you have no idea how long I've waited for this moment. You, wanting advice on clothes. Wait, hold on." Rita waved a hand Sarah's way. "I need a moment. I'm all verklempt."

"This is serious."

"Sorry." Rita made a show of composing her features. "There. I'm ready now. So what's the occasion? Job interview?"

Sarah squirmed.

"So…. Not a job interview." Rita tapped a finger to her chin, pretending confusion. "What else could you possibly want new clothes for, Sarah?" She paused overlong. "Unless it's to attract a guy's attention."

Sarah sank into the chair alongside Rita. "I'm no good at this kind of thing."

Rita laughed. "Oh, honey, we're all good at it. Some of us just have more practice than others. And I'm glad to lend you a little of my expertise."

"Before the festival?" Everyone took part in the upcoming town festival. The busyness of festival week offered the area towns a chance to come together for a long weekend of welcoming visitors, family and friends.

Rita stood. "How's now?"

Sarah smiled, relieved. "Perfect."

"What about the red?"

Rita studied the combination Sarah held up, then frowned. "Trying too hard."

"That's not something."

"Just part of the game," Rita replied. "Besides, Craig's already interested. You want clothes that say he's got plenty of reason to be attracted, but subtle. And this is a fool's chase, anyway. The guy's smitten."

Sarah remembered the look on his face when she left him with Lady. Closed. Shuttered. "Just in case you're wrong, I want something that says I know how to step out of barn boots when necessary."

Rita grinned. "Can't argue that. What about the gold?"

Sarah slipped into the fitted, ribbed top. The cut-in neckline showed plenty of shoulder.

"Perfect with your skin and hair," Rita told her. "Your shell necklace would go great with it, too. And that earthy wrap-around skirt. The short one."

Sarah fingered the soft folds, the muted colors welcoming

fall, then eyed the growing pile to her left. "I haven't spent this much on clothing since…ever."

Rita laughed. "Then it's about time. And try this scarf as a belt. No. Lower on the hip."

"Lower?"

Rita rolled her eyes. "Here. Let me."

Sarah stared at the reflection in the mirror. "What do you think?"

Rita met her gaze through the looking glass. "I think Craig Macklin's dead in the water."

"Really?"

"Indubitably. This outfit says one thing and one thing only."

Sarah was almost afraid to ask. "And that is?"

"Wow."

Brett and Craig stood side by side when Sarah pulled into the drive. Both faces turned her way, one looking hurt and lost, the other—

She tried not to read too much into what she saw in Craig's gold-flecked eyes. The approving appraisal took him long seconds to mask as she moved across the yard. "Hey, guys. What's up?"

Brett stayed quiet, the sting of the soccer rejection still raw. Craig took the reins. "The annual fishing derby is coming up during the festival. I want to enter Brett and me in the competition."

"Together?" Sarah looked up at him. Big mistake. No way could she hide the feelings she harbored when he was right there, flesh and blood, looking too good to be believed in jeans and a roughed-up Syracuse T-shirt. Flecks of pale paint dotted the thinning knit, almost transparent in places after no small number of washes.

Talk about a rock and a hard place. Looking up, she faced his eyes, the steady gaze that saw into her heart. Her soul. Facing straight on, she got a close-up view of cotton-draped chest, broad and brawny. Muscular arms whose sharp definition showed the work of building houses and tending animals. Trouble, either way.

She glanced up.

Head tilted, he watched her. A tiny smile edged his mouth as his left eye narrowed, then relaxed. A glint of amusement made brighter flecks stand out in his light-brown eyes.

"They've got various categories," he answered, rocking back on his heels. "Age groups and pairs. There's a mixed doubles grouping as well. You like to fish, Sarah?"

The innocent question sent her heart pounding. She hazarded a glance into his eyes. "I'd like to learn."

Amusement turned to tenderness in a heartbeat. "I expect you're a fast learner."

She stepped back, literally and figuratively, refocusing on Brett. "Um, not that fast. You and Brett are entering together?"

"I dunno." Brett sounded worn. Sarah elbowed him.

"You like to fish, right?"

"Yeah."

"And you've got Doc ready to pay the entry fee?"

"I guess."

"So what's to wonder? You've got precious little summer left, kid. Enjoy it. Can I come watch?" Again she lifted her face to Craig's. This time he grinned.

"I'd like that. If you don't disturb us, that is." He tried to make his face serious, but failed. She laughed at his efforts.

"Promise. I'm helping at the sheep products booth during the festival, so I probably won't get time to pester you boys." Her heart soared when Craig looked disappointed. "But I'll be glad to watch you grab first prize."

"People come from all over for this derby," Craig explained, dubious. "The prize is a twenty thousand dollar bass boat. I'd be happy with a fifty-dollar check and a box of new hooks."

"Me too." Brett sided with his friend in quick fashion.

"You've got to dream, boys," Sarah reminded them. "Reach for the stars."

"Did you up your meds without medical permission?" Craig demanded, feigning concern.

Brett looked confused. Sarah grinned, then turned, looking over the simple property that bore her name. A dream come true for a young woman, a shepherd. "Nope. Just learning to go for the gold."

"Are you now?" His tone showed a definite upswing.

She nodded and headed for the stairs, various shopping bags clutched in her hands. "Most assuredly."

Craig spotted his grandmother's wide-brimmed summer hat in the lodge vegetable garden and headed her way. "Need help?"

She turned and smiled to see him, then eyed the peck baskets dotting the row. "I'd love it. I enjoy picking, but carrying baskets is no big treat these days."

"That bursitis still bothering your shoulder?"

She sent him a wizened look. "Only when the humidity's up or there's a storm brewing. Best barometer in St. Lawrence County."

Craig laughed, then sobered. "Grams, I need to talk with you. About the festival next week."

She nodded, eyes down, her aged hands gently plucking pickling cukes from broad-leafed vines. "What's up?"

"I'm entering the fishing derby."

She nodded. "Good plan. Your grandpa always said you were the most natural fisherman he'd ever seen. Got it from his daddy, he'd say."

"With Brett Slocum," Craig continued. "Tom's son."

Grams rocked back on her heels and peered up at him. "Do tell."

"He's been living with Sarah, across the street from my new place."

She nodded, making the connection.

"And he's been helping me with the house. Doing this and that. Odd jobs."

"And you're worried how I might take this?" Grams' expression said his worries were unfounded.

Craig didn't try to hide his relief. "I wanted to be upfront with you. Not surprise you while you helped at the baked goods booth."

Grams pursed her lips and stood. Craig reached out a hand to help her balance. She faced him square, her jaw set. "Craig, I loved your grandpa. Loved him to distraction. He was a good man, a good father, a strong partner. He loved God and loved me, and worked hard. What more could a woman ask?"

Craig shrugged. "I think that about sums it up, right?"

She narrowed her gaze and looked off, beyond him, then brought her focus back, brows drawn. "But he wasn't perfect, Craig. Like the rest of us, Grandpa had his weaknesses. A little too headstrong, too impetuous. That business with Tom Slocum, the investments."

Dread filled Craig's heart. His soul. His belly filled with an anchor weight of guilt.

"Grandpa never had extra money to play with, but he loved to study the market, see what was going on in the big leagues. When his retirement turned over and we got the check for selling the old house, he went a little crazy. Plum over the top."

Dread sucked Craig's air. Meeting Grams' earnest look, he knew it was time to confess his part in the whole mess. "I encouraged him, Grams."

Her brow wrinkled deeper, puzzled.

"When he talked about investing the whole thing, I told him to go big or go home," Craig confessed. "He laughed and said I was a chip off the old block, and then went ahead and did it." Craig shook his head, sorry to have to confess his stupidity but glad to finally have it off his chest. "I've been sorry ever since."

Grams grasped his arm. "You think you influenced him?"

Craig nodded. "I know I did."

Grams tilted her head, her face a blend of concern and empathy. "Craig, no one talked your Grandpa into anything, ever. I was married to the man for nearly fifty years, and Heaven knows I couldn't sway him one way or the other once his mind was made up. You didn't push him to invest that money." She shook her head, decisive. "And I couldn't talk him out of it, though I tried. In the end, Tom did us wrong, but your grandpa knew better. He just couldn't resist finally having some money to invest, a chance to play the market. Run with the big dogs."

"But—"

Her grip tightened on his arm. "Tom did us wrong, no two ways about that, but Grandpa shouldn't have gone into this so shortsighted. Trusting. There's plenty of blame to go around, and none of it's yours."

"But I—"

"No." Grams' firm tone left no room for discussion. "I loved your grandpa, but I knew his weak spots. He made this decision on his own. It had nothing whatsoever to do with you, regardless of what you might have said or done. I mean that."

The weight Craig had carried for years eased.

Grams motioned to the baskets. She grasped one while Craig manned the other two. "On top of that, there's no time like the present to put all of this to rest. Put it behind us. I'm going to call Rita Slocum and see if she'd help us out with the baked goods booth. No one holds a candle to that woman when it comes to baking, and if we can offer some of her creations, we'll have record sales. This year's earnings are going towards the new hospice facility in Canton."

"You wouldn't mind working with Rita?" Craig asked.

"Not in the least," declared Grams. "I'm old enough to realize that people shouldn't be held accountable for the actions of anyone other than themselves. I'll call her now, see what she says. It would be good for all concerned to have her there, don't you think?"

"Yes." Craig set the pickles down and grabbed Grams into a big hug, his turmoil eased by her commonsense directives. "Yes, it would."

Chapter Twenty-Five

Sarah handed the phone to Rita, unable to hide her surprise. "It's Cora Macklin."

Rita paled.

Sarah extended the phone, nudging Rita with her look.

Gulping, Rita took the phone, a slight tremor moving her fingers. "Hello?"

Sarah couldn't hear Cora's end of the conversation, but Rita's responses clued her in. She'd called to invite Rita's help in the baked goods booth at the festival.

Sarah's heart stutter-stepped, afraid this was too much, too soon, and half scared the gesture was too little, too late.

"I...umm..."

Rita nodded, listening. Slowly, her frown eased. "I could handle those at my place."

Her tone sounded hopeful. Almost normal. Sarah breathed deep, watching, waiting, unsure what to expect. What to do. The mix of emotions made her realize she'd been emulating Brett and Livvie's behavior, protecting Rita from anything that might nudge her off the wagon.

"Well..." Rita hesitated, thinking. "We could do a selection of background cakes to augment what others donate. Pounds, layers, small sheet cakes that we can price affordably and still make a decent profit. How would that be?"

Cora's answer must have been positive because a small smile softened Rita's jaw, her cheeks. A moment later, she shadowed. "Cora, are you sure about this? Really sure?"

Cora's response had Rita breathing a sigh of relief, the shadow disappearing. "I'll see you Thursday night for setup. And Cora? Thank you."

Rita sent Sarah a nervous smile as she handed her the phone. "You heard."

"Yes."

"You think it's crazy?"

"I think it's wonderful. And way past time." She met Rita's look and couldn't help but ask, "Are you ready, Reet?"

Rita swept the room with a look, her gaze taking in the late summer day, the thinning light, the country sounds of a settled evening. "My ovens have been cold for way too long, Sarah. It's way past time to fire things up."

Sarah grinned. "Dibs on the first carrot cake."

Rita slanted her a teasing look. "Only if you pay up, Wise Woman. We're supporting a good cause here. No handouts."

Sarah laughed. "I'll bring along the little I didn't spend on new clothes," she replied. "Make the carrot cake small, okay? Affordable."

Rita's chin came up, her shoulders straighter. Firmer. "Will do."

"What's the leaderboard look like?" Sarah counted on Ben Waters' height to see above the press of people surrounding the weigh station Friday evening.

"Some guys from Michigan are in first in the large mouth doubles category. They've been on the *Deborah I.*"

A Macklin entry. Craig's dad knew area waterways. He was a woodsman's woodsman and had turned his love of nature into sound provisions for his family. His lodge thrived with business, his knowledge of North Country hunting and fishing almost legendary.

"Second is some fellas from Erie. Third I can't read because some woman's wearin' a hat that could shade an opry singer and leave room for friends. Fourth is your boyfriend and nephew."

"Ben." Sarah chastised him with a look but couldn't quite hide her pleasure.

"Tell me he ain't." The old man looked down and grinned before he turned back. "Thought as much."

Fourth. Not bad for a guy and a kid in a rowboat. Craig seemed accustomed to the good-natured teasing that went along with his low-investment fishing style amidst the huge expenditures laid out around him. His attire screamed local yokel, his flannel shirt waving open over the worn T-shirt beneath, his battle-scarred baseball cap completing the image. There wasn't a vestige of doctor apparent.

"It gives a false sense of superiority," he assured Sarah when she rolled her eyes at him that evening. His glance indicated the mass of fishermen waiting for their official weights. "Designer polos don't belong on fishing boats. It goes against nature."

"Isn't there a happy medium?" she asked, raking his clothes a look before laughing at his manufactured hurt expression. "Casual *and* cool?"

"This from a woman who runs a sheep farm in overalls and barn boots." When she dropped her chin, he tipped it back up, his glance skimming her cute skirt and rib-knit top. "You clean up real nice, Miss Slocum."

Was it the look or the words that made her feel so good? Probably both. "So do you," she admitted with a grin. "Though it's a rare occasion."

"We'll remedy that next week," he promised, his fingers grazing her chin. "A night out, you and me. Dinner. Romance." He grinned and winked. "Wednesday?"

"Craig." The combination of his touch and his words flustered her, making her want to move forward, into his embrace. Unfortunately a wooden counter lay between them, stocked with mittens, socks and hats.

Still, a date, at long last—

She blushed, thinking of it.

"I've got to round up Brett," said Craig, regretful. He let one finger trace the heat of her cheek, his manner intent. He leaned close, rubbing her ear, her temple with his whiskered cheek, the textured feel of his beard-roughened skin a sweet pleasure. Sarah was pretty sure fishing wasn't topping his priority list as he stepped back, his gaze lowering to her mouth, lingering. He sighed. "He was snagging freebies at the baked goods booth. This has been really good for her," Craig acknowledged, shifting his look across the green to where Rita and various other women boxed and sold delicious confections.

The sight of Cora Macklin and Rita Slocum working together had drawn more than one curious look, but the two women had found common ground.

Thank You, God.

"It has." Sarah swallowed her mixed feelings. She welcomed Rita's return to strength, but her house seemed wanting as the kids spent more time with their mother.

Something in her voice shifted Craig's attention. His expression turned curious. "You okay?"

She mustered a smile. "Fine."

"Hmm." His look said he wasn't quite buying it. He glanced around, eyeing the bustle surrounding them, and chose not to pursue the topic. Sarah breathed a sigh of relief, but the restlessness returned as she watched him stride away, his step quick and sure.

Etta Waters stopped Craig as he cut across the festival site. "I haven't seen you favor the festival this much in years," she crowed, beaming.

He didn't pretend to misunderstand her good-natured teasing. "A good year all around."

"I'll say." She nodded, brisk. "And we've never been privy to so much action at the sheep booth before. It's positively hopping over there."

Craig's interest spiked. "How's that?"

"Well there's you, of course." Etta smiled and patted his arm with a touch of comfort. "And Marc DeHollander has stopped by more than once, if you know what I mean." Raising her hand, she pretended to count. "That nice new science teacher from Potsdam's been by every day. Twice today, actually. And Brooks Harriman."

"You're a troublemaker, Etta Waters."

She giggled.

"If it were up to you," Craig continued, "I'd be challenging my best friend to a duel, ruining a guy's chances for tenure and rendering the town's woodcrafter's hands useless. Gossip can be an evil thing."

She nodded, her dark eyes sparkling. "And since when is reporting facts considered gossip?"

She had him there. He glanced from the woolens booth to Etta. "Busier than last year?"

"Tenfold."

Craig scanned the growing crowd and spotted Marc alongside the Ladies Auxiliary lemonade booth. He headed that way. Marc held out a hand as he approached. "Craig. How's it going? Can I buy you one?" He nodded toward the overblown picture of a smiling yellow lemon.

"Absolutely. And everything's fine. How about you?"

Marc glanced around, affable. "Doing okay. Great festival."

"It is." Staring his buddy down, Craig accepted the lemonade.

Marc gestured to the leaderboard. "I was surprised to see your name with Brett Slocum's."

"Good kid."

Marc accepted his response in typical fashion. "I'm sure he is. But I was still surprised."

"He's been staying with Sarah," Craig rejoined. He folded his arms across his chest and braced his legs apart, his look level.

"With Sarah?" Repeating the words, Marc leaned back, his jaw working, his voice thoughtful, eyeing Craig's posture.

"I understand you've developed an increased interest in sheep products?"

As the light dawned, Marc grinned. "Let's say I had an increased interest. It's just been downsized. Who'd have thought?" Laughing, he clapped Craig on the back.

Craig relaxed his stance. "Not me, certainly. Now?" He rubbed a hand across his chin, eyeing the slender figure in the woolens booth, her braid shifting as she interacted with customers. "I can't imagine life without her."

"Oh, man. You do have it bad." Marc offered him a look of commiseration. "Couldn't keep the three-date rule, huh?"

Admitting this made him feel like a first-class heel. "We haven't actually dated yet," Craig confessed.

"You're kidding."

"Nope."

"Macklin, you're pathetic."

"Or really good," Craig supposed with a grin. "Either way, she's off the market."

"Message delivered," Marc acknowledged, smiling in Sarah's direction. "She's a wonderful girl. After all that's happened, you're lucky she gives you the time of day."

"Don't remind me. I've improved."

Marc angled him a glance and nodded. "I can't disagree. Do I get to be a groomsman?"

"Absolutely." Relaxing, Craig took a long draw from his tumbler. "But let me ask her first."

"You sure she'll say yes?"

Watching Sarah, Craig raised his cup to Marc's and shook his head. "Not at all. But I'll ask her anyway. Some things are worth the risk."

Marc contemplated that and shrugged. Craig grinned. "Your turn's coming, DeHollander. Man doesn't live by beef alone."

The reference to Marc's herd drew his laugh. "It's worked so far," he retorted, grinning. "Besides, you just snagged the most eligible farm wife candidate. There aren't many girls like Sarah. Faith-filled. Smart. Beautiful. Unafraid to get dirty."

"You're close to getting punched again," Craig warned. Marc laughed and slapped an arm around Craig's shoulders.

"I'm happy for you, old man."

Craig nodded, his heart pinching at the sight of Sarah bouncing someone's baby as the young mother shopped for winter gloves. "Me, too. If she says yes."

Chapter Twenty-Six

Sarah pulled her rain slicker close as the north wind channeled beneath the barn's eaves. The late-summer day hinted fall, the wet chill a portent of what was to come.

She never minded winter. It was a given when you lived at the forty-fifth latitude. In fact, she welcomed the cold, the peace of the winter season, the flurry of spring, summer and fall work behind her.

But this year the change of seasons loomed stark. It heightened the sudden silence of her house with Rita and the kids gone, the family court judge approving Rita's petition for custody. By Wednesday, Sarah felt twitchy.

The festival weekend left a chain of pleasant memories, including the thrill of seeing Craig and Brett receive third prize in the final tally. The boy's confidence had surged with the two hundred dollars' worth of fishing tackle he claimed as a yellow ribbon winner. Sarah relished the victory, coming so soon after the soccer defeat, knowing Craig engineered the entry for just that reason.

And Craig?

Her heart did a hop, skip and jump at the thought of her rangy neighbor. He'd been working double time since the weekend, making up for the days he'd taken off.

The promised date didn't look hopeful. As she gathered

inoculation supplies, she checked her phone messages, hoping to hear his voice.

Nope. The single voice mail came from the wrong guy. The science teacher's attentions made the old axiom about raining and pouring ring true. Sarah turned, supplies in hand, as the phone rang. She answered it with one eye on the clock. "Hello."

"Sarah? It's Craig."

His voice drew a smile. "I was just thinking about you."

"Anything good?" He sounded rushed.

"Pretty much," she confessed. She heard him draw a deep breath. When he spoke again, his voice held relief.

"I miss you. Taking time off for the festival was great, but it totally messed up our office schedule. I'll be marking time here for the next two days at least, which kills our date plans."

"You sound tired."

"A little." She heard him take a long drink of something. "Hungry, mostly, but I've got an incoming critical canine. The repair will take a while, if he survives the transport. Then he'll most likely need post-surgical monitoring. I tried calling a little while ago to explain, but your line was busy."

"You must have called when that new teacher from Potsdam was calling."

"And he wanted?" Craig's voice went from apologetic to stern.

"I have no idea," Sarah replied, her fingers toying with the buttons on the phone. "He left a message."

"That said?"

Sarah grinned and replied, "That he couldn't get my coffee-colored eyes out of his mind and would I like to have dinner this weekend?"

Craig muttered something less than proper in a tone two steps below a growl. Sarah heard the jangle of the waiting room door as someone arrived at the clinic. "Honey, gotta go." Craig's voice was back to business. "Talk to you later."

By the time Sarah had administered her necessary injections, an hour had passed. Glancing at her watch, she hurried upstairs to shower and change.

Maybe they couldn't go out for the romantic evening he'd promised, but she could salvage time with Craig if she hustled. And the guy had to eat, right? By the time she pulled into the clinic's parking lot forty minutes later, the smell of fresh-baked pizza from a local shop had her mouth watering.

The rear door of the clinic stood ajar. The window blinds angled left, out of kilter. She nudged the door shut and carried the food through a back hall she'd never seen before, listening for sounds.

Muffled sobs came from the waiting room. Sarah set the food in the small kitchen area and moved toward the sound.

State troopers filled the room. A woman sat next to one, her cheeks wet, the officer's arm snugged around her shoulders. Red-rimmed eyes were the norm in an area filled with robust men, the sort that didn't get misty-eyed easily. Sarah stopped in the doorway, uncertain. The trooper holding the woman looked up. "Any news?"

Sarah shook her head. "No. I'm sorry. I'm a friend of Dr. Macklin's. Is it your dog?"

The man sank back. "My partner, Kip. He took a bullet meant for me." The woman cried harder, fear mingling with grief.

Instinctively, Sarah moved forward, aware of the men watching. She stooped and grasped the woman's hands. "Can we pray?"

The woman straightened.

Sarah sensed the mixed looks around her. Eyes closed, she took the woman's hand and reached out her second hand in blind faith. Fingers clasped hers, the touch reassuring. "Our Father, who art in Heaven, hallowed be Thy Name…"

The joint effort resounded throughout the small room. As they brought the ancient words to a close, Sarah offered her own entreaty, asking God's blessings on the doctors' knowledgeable hands and Kip's spirit.

Her prayer broke the ice. In voices ranging from wavering

to angry, the room filled with troopers' petitions. As prayer rounded the chairs, peace descended. Fear lessened. Anger dissipated.

Silence blanketed the room. Sarah held the woman's hand, letting her prayer rise from her heart, unwilling to disturb the pervading quiet. When she opened her eyes, Craig stood in the doorway. He crossed the room to the couple on the couch. "There's hope."

"Thank You, God."

The woman squeezed Sarah's hand, then released it to hug the man beside her. Craig's eyes softened when he saw Sarah. He reached down to pull her upright. It wasn't the time for words, she knew that. Pressing her fingers, Craig addressed the group. "The bullet did major damage. It tore through Kip, causing massive internal trauma and breaking his left hind leg. We're not out of the woods yet," he cautioned, "but there's hope. We were able to stabilize him with Oxyglobin until the donor blood arrived. Without that medication—" Craig shook his head, his hand tensing "—there would have been no chance."

"But now there is?" The woman stood on unsteady legs, her eyes imploring. "He might live?"

"The next twelve hours are critical," Craig told her. "I'm staying with him tonight. I'll intervene if necessary. He's a beautiful animal."

"Belgian Malinois," explained one of the officers. "He and Mike have been partners for over three years. The dog's a solid cop."

High praise indeed. Craig waved his hand. "You're welcome to sleep here, though it's not comfortable. I've got the numbers you gave me." He turned and addressed the couple. "If there's any change, I'll call you. And if you've got kids at home, they're probably worried sick."

"He's right," agreed Mike. He stepped closer to his wife. "We'll go home, Doc, but it's nearly forty minutes away. You'll call us if—" He couldn't say the words. His eyes spoke for him.

"Absolutely. Any change at all, I'll be on the phone," Craig promised. He reached out a hand. "Keep praying."

His words brought several pairs of eyes Sarah's way. One of the troopers grasped her hand. "Thank you, Miss. It helped."

"Yeah." Another officer grabbed her in a hug. "Thanks."

One by one they thanked both Sarah and Craig until the waiting room stood empty. Quiet.

Craig turned her to face him, his eyes quizzical. "What exactly did you do out here?"

"Prayed with them," she told him, leaning forward to rest her head against his chest. "They were so angry. I thought it might help."

"I'll say." Leaning back, he tipped her chin up, his head tilted, his expression gentle. "You came."

She nodded, loving the look of him, the feel, the way his eyes softened when he looked at her. "Yes."

"Because?"

"You needed me."

He hugged her, dropping his cheek to her hair. She felt the weariness in him, alongside the joy. "Thank you. What about the teacher guy?"

Sarah smiled up at him, hoping her eyes said more than her words. "Who?"

He grinned. "Right answer." He led her to the recovery area, where Hank and Ralph were cleaning up from the intervention. "Boys. We've got company."

"And food," she announced, angling her head toward the access hall as she moved to the dog's side. "There's pizza in the kitchen."

Ralph and Hank exchanged glances. "If he doesn't marry her, I will," Ralph declared.

Sarah laughed as she stroked the Belgian's thick-furred head. "You're already married," she scolded, her voice soft, her touch light.

"It might be worth the hassle to get the food," the older man responded with a grin.

Sarah scanned his ample proportions and sent him a look of disbelief. "I don't think access is the problem you make it out to be."

"Gotcha." Hank laughed at Ralph, then grinned at Sarah while he washed. "Come on, Ralph. Let's grab some pizza and leave these youngsters to the overnight. I'm beat."

Craig shook Hank's hand. He nodded to the dog, intentionally sedated to allow his body recovery time. "I couldn't have done it without you."

"Me either," agreed Hank, giving Craig's hand a solid pump. "Too many holes. Amazing what a single bullet can do. I think he'll do okay." They watched as Sarah put her cheek to the dog's neck, nuzzling, her voice crooning something low and native. She closed her eyes, blocking them out, her words for the dog alone.

"You're a lucky man, Doc." Ralph's voice tinged with admiration. Sarah let a little smile curve her lips.

"Blessed," Craig corrected. She heard the scrape of a chair as he moved one closer to the injured dog. "Definitely blessed."

Chapter Twenty-Seven

Sarah stirred at the sound of a closing door. She strove to move deeper into the pillow. A gentle hand stopped her. "Sarah. Wake up. It's almost morning."

"Hmm?" Disoriented, she blinked and yawned. "What?"

"Sarah."

The deep voice raised her senses. Blinking again, she focused on Craig. "Hey. What are…?" As memories tweaked, she looked around, regaining her bearings. "I fell asleep?"

Craig laughed. "About ten minutes after you put your cheek to Kip's neck. Approximately," he scanned his watch, "seven hours ago."

"No." Embarrassed, she looked up at him. "I meant to stay up with you. Keep watch."

Craig laid a gentle hand alongside her cheek. "You kept him calm. As long as you were there, his vitals stayed steady. You were his best medicine, Wise Woman."

"Really?" The idea pleased her. Hank slipped in, tugging on a clean scrub coat. "What now?"

"Next shift," answered Hank with a smile. "Go home, guys. Get some sleep." He didn't notice Sarah's look of chagrin. She, at least, wasn't a bit tired.

"Come on." Craig put an arm around her shoulders. "Let's get you home. I need a nap if I'm going to be useful today."

She reached up a hand to his bristly cheek. "You stayed awake all night?"

He nodded and stretched. "You're pretty when you sleep." He smiled at her reaction, then headed for the door, swinging it open so she could step through. "But you're downright beautiful when you're awake."

Sarah looked around in surprise as Craig's SUV mounted his angled drive. "I thought you were dropping me home."

"I'll walk you over shortly. It's time you saw my house."

"Now? You're dead on your feet. I'll see it later."

"Now." His tone left no room for argument. She gave him a funny look, but unfastened her seatbelt and stepped out of the car. "Beautiful view, Doc." She waved a hand to the broad vista before her. The back broadened into an expansive site, the lot spreading far and wide. Lovely.

Craig shrugged. "I prefer the front."

Sarah turned, puzzled. "But the trees block most of that. All you can see is some of my pasture and my barn."

He gave her a look meant to curl her toes and hoped it did. "That's right."

She flushed. He smiled to see it, then led her inside. "Come on. You've put this off long enough."

He opened a back door that led into a service area. A full bath opened to her left and a laundry room to her right. He nodded to the closets and cupboards lining the walls. "My work gets messy. I wanted to be able to get rid of dirty clothes and shower right here."

"Smart," she agreed. "I hate that I have to trek through the house and clomp upstairs in dirty clothes to reach the tub. Old houses didn't have setups like this."

He nudged her forward. "The kitchen."

"Oh, my."

Golden oak cabinets brought the honeyed tone of post and beam construction into the room. Red-veined ivory granite counters reflected the spiced tones of the patterned tile floor. A three-sided bay featuring a centered door allowed extra floor space for a table and access to the backyard. The kitchen and dining area both overlooked the panoramic view. She turned to Craig, amazed. "You picked the ideal setting for this house. How on earth did you do that?"

"I had help." He smiled, leading her forward. He saw no sense admitting that left to his own devices he might not have purchased the land if he'd known Sarah was his closest neighbor.

But God knew. As sure as Craig was that he'd come home to the future God planned for him, he couldn't say he'd have understood the possibilities six months previous. "The credit goes to divine intervention," he continued, drawing her into the living room.

The soft carpet invited repose. Bending, Sarah stirred her fingers through the thick fibers. "Great density."

"I used to play on the floor with Rocket," he told her, smiling. "Now Lady chases my socks."

"I'll bet she loves that. What's this?" She crossed the room and lifted a wooden carving from the mantel. Her expression waxed from appreciative to puzzled. She turned Craig's way, the piece raised up. "A white fawn."

He nodded, holding her gaze. "Yes."

The pale baby nuzzled the underside of the taupe-toned deer, rooting for food while the mother gave licks of attention to the fawn's neck. It was an intimate look at mother and child, accepted regardless of their obvious differences.

"I ordered it for you. From Hy Everts."

Sarah studied the exquisite detail. From the muscle definition of the doe's withers to the almost visible quiver of the fawn's tail, the piece was nature, captured in wood. "It's wonderful."

Craig stepped forward. "I wanted something different. Something special for you, so you'd know that none of the controversy mattered anymore. Once I got to know you, I realized how stupid I'd been. I wanted to make it up to you."

Her lip trembled. She held the carved figure lightly, studying the mother-child configuration, her fingers caressing the doe's smooth head. Craig's hands closed over hers. Looking up, she met his gaze. "It's beautiful, Craig. It reminds me of my mother."

He smiled.

"Do I get to take it home?"

"Not yet. Come see the rest."

Sarah set the statue back in place and reached for his hand. "I'm all yours."

Grasping her fingers, he prayed the expression was more than just a casual phrase and led her up the open stairs. "There's a bedroom downstairs," he waved to the left, "in front of the laundry room/bathroom combo. This is the loft." He watched her eyes wander the open area. "I thought it would make a great alternative sleeping area. Maybe a futon or sleep sofa that can be used as a bed when necessary. What do you think?"

She smiled up at him. "I think you're right. Something in earth tones, to pull up that shade of brick red from downstairs. I love that you kept the wood light. Dark, heavy woods can be overbearing in the winter."

He nodded, pulling her forward once again. "Bedrooms here and here. Bath. Master bedroom." Stepping in, he hit a switch. Soft light infused the space, illuminating the furnishings. A massive Adirondack log bed centered the room, its rugged qualities a focal point. To the left were closets, large and roomy. To the right, a dresser and chest of drawers. Then a master bath. Eyeing the double fixtures, she turned back to him. "It's gorgeous, Craig. Perfect."

He made a face. "Not quite. Something's missing."

"Oh?" She turned, eyeing the room. The near windows overlooked the pond site below. The far windows embraced forestland. She turned, her forehead furrowed. "Well, it needs curtains. And bedding. Touches of color here and there. But it's wonderful."

"It's got potential," he agreed, drawing her back. He slipped his arms around her from behind, surveying the room. Touched his lips to her hair before he shifted them to her ear. "But I'm no good with that color stuff," he said softly. "What would you suggest?"

She leaned against the strength of his chest, his arms, as if she belonged there, feeling too right, too natural not to belong there. "The bed's rugged, so I'd soften it with light colors. A little red to continue that thread, but I'd pick a comforter that brings spring into the room year-round. Maybe yellows and greens with sprigs of red." Tilting her head she glanced up at him. "I'd use a soft window covering. Curtains, not drapes. Probably swagged to open the view but diffuse the light."

"When can we shop?"

She turned, surprised. "You want me to shop with you?"

"Oh, yeah." He dropped his mouth to hers and languished in the kiss he'd longed for, feeling her melt into the embrace, the beat of his heart against hers. "And then I want you to share it with me. Marry me. Thread all the red you want to, honey, as long as I come home to find you waiting for me every night."

"Craig…" Her gaze shot up, mouth open, surprised.

"I love you, Sarah. Marry me. Please."

She stepped back, hands to her cheeks. Craig watched her, waiting.

"You're sure?" Her voice wasn't the strong, self-assured Abenaki tone she'd mastered over the years. It was soft, hesitant, but filled with hope.

"Real sure." He stepped forward, smiling. "How about you?"

"I—"

"Oh, wait. I almost forgot." Grabbing her hand, he led her back through the loft, down the stairs, around the corner, through the kitchen and service areas to the garage beyond. "Come here."

Still tugging, he guided her through the second garage bay to the back door, then made her close her eyes before she stepped through. "Okay," he told her. "Open your eyes."

"Craig." Kenneled beyond the garage was Lady, the fast-growing Border Collie she'd offered him in trade. Alongside were two Shetland ewes, soft and round. One was moorit-toned, a blend of browns and blacks. The other was red, her wavy hair glinting copper in the angled rays of the morning sun. "Craig."

Sarah turned, her eyes wet with unshed tears. He gathered her in, feeling her chest heave with emotion. "Hey. Hey. I didn't mean to make you cry. I just thought it would be a good time to start that side flock. Give you spinning wool. You like them?" Nudging her away, he leaned down to catch her eye. "Pretty colors, huh?"

"Beautiful." She reached up for his kiss, then burrowed her head into his chest once more. "Yes."

He frowned. "Yes?"

She raised her face to his, then looped her hands around his neck. "You asked me a question upstairs. The answer is yes."

Craig laughed. "Honey, I knew that."

"Really?" She angled her head, eyeing him.

"I figured if the kitchen didn't do it, the bedroom would," he teased, letting his eyes twinkle in amusement. "The sheep were just frosting on the cake."

"You're still cocky." She watched him a long moment, then launched herself into his arms, laughing. "I love it."

"And me?" Kissing her once more, he set her down with care and studied her face, his hand caressing the side that had been damaged. "Do you love me, Sarah?"

"Oh, Craig." She drew a deep breath and put a hand up over his. "How could you possibly not know? With all my heart."

A load he hadn't known he carried eased away. "I asked your father for your hand."

Surprise and dismay vied for her features. "Ouch. How did that go?"

"Like you'd expect," Craig told her, his hands cradling her face. He narrowed his eyes and angled his head, wanting her to understand why he'd approached Tom Sr. at all, but unwilling to give her the details of a conversation best left unspoken. "I didn't want anything to stand in our way. You understand that, don't you?"

"I do."

He grinned at the prophetic words. "Music to my ears, Wise Woman. Let's set a date."

"Aren't you tired?" She traced her fingers along the curve of his jaw, his neck. "You haven't slept."

"I'll sleep," he promised, drawing her back inside. He grabbed a calendar from the wall near the phone. "Pick."

She pointed to the first Saturday of October. "The leaves will be beautiful then."

She surprised him, but he wasn't about to argue. "Five weeks. Can we do it?"

She nodded. "Small. Cozy. I'm not a big wedding kind of girl, Doc."

"You're sure? You only get to do this once."

She nodded, smiling. "I'm sure." Taking his hands into hers, she threw him a curve. "But before we go any farther, we need to talk about family."

"We just did. My parents are ecstatic and your father is informed. About the best we can hope for at this point."

She shook her head. "I mean our family." She gazed up at him, her look intent. "I want children."

He read the future in her eyes. His heart swelled. "Me, too. As soon as possible and as many as you're willing to have," he answered immediately.

"I wouldn't mind a little time alone with you first," she confessed, flushing.

"I see potential in that," he agreed, grinning. The hand around her waist tugged her closer. "Great potential, in fact."

"But then I want a noisy house," she warned, teasing. "Babies, puppies and the occasional lamb that needs warming."

"It's a good thing I built big," he answered, dropping his mouth to hers once more. "And that the lowest level is meant to be finished and useful. I'm ready to fill it whenever you are, honey."

She met his kiss with one in return. "We'll discuss it on the honeymoon."

His face creased. "Now, that's a problem. There's no way I'll get time off next month. I've used up my vacation working on the house and fishing." He gestured to the home around them with a wave of his hand. "Is that okay?"

Sarah's gaze wandered the home. "Can't we just honeymoon here?" She raised big brown eyes to his. "Play house?"

The thought of playing house with Sarah had him wishing time away in fast forward. "I'd love to play house with you, Mrs. Macklin." He smiled at her reaction to the name, then fished in his pocket. From a small brown velvet case he removed a ring. "This was my grandmother's," he told her, holding it out. "She left it to me. If you don't like it, we can shop for another. Or have it reset."

The faceted diamond flashed in a deep gold setting, surrounded by pierced openwork. Tiny diamonds channeled thin gold lines, a sparkling metallic lacework. The antique ring offered old world beauty. Sarah held out her hand. "We won't change a thing," she declared, smiling as he slipped the ring into place. "It's perfect, Craig."

Craig slipped his arms around her, catching her mouth in a kiss of betrothal. "My sentiments exactly."

* * * * *

Want more amazing North Country series?
Watch for Rita and Brooks' story in
MADE TO ORDER FAMILY,
coming in September 2010
from Love Inspired.

Dear Reader,

Adult choices are often inspired by childhood dreams.

My favorite childhood book was *Understand Betsy*, by Dorothy Canfield Fisher, a poignant story of a pampered girl's coming of age on a working farm. Cousin Ann's child-raising concepts inspired my own mothering techniques.

Years ago my mother related a story of three small children who lost their parents. Despite having a big family, these children ended up in foster care.

As a mother and former foster care provider, the idea that no one stepped forward to take these children broke my heart. How I wish there had been an Aunt Sarah to help, or a Cousin Ann, a family member to embrace these children, make them their own.

More than ever families need to support one another in our busy, disjointed, technologically advanced society. Simple things like sharing a meal, a story, a walk or a chore mean so much to a yearning child. In this story Sarah recognizes a need and fills it, determined to do the right thing despite her dysfunctional family history.

I'd love to hear your stories, thoughts and opinions. Feel free to visit me at ruthloganherne.com or e-mail me at logan-herne@gmail.com. If you prefer snail mail, drop me a line care of Steeple Hill Books, 233 Broadway, Suite 1001, New York, NY 10279. I look forward to hearing from you.

Ruthy

QUESTIONS FOR DISCUSSION

1. Sarah returns to the North Country to help Rita and the kids after her brother's death. Given her family dynamics, it's a huge sacrifice that shows little initial promise. Have you ever experienced that kind of reluctant change, only to have wonderful things happen as a result?

2. Craig's affinity for pretty girls nicks Sarah's self-confidence. Her self-image is warped by her brothers' emotional abuse. How can we help young people maintain a good self-image in spite of their surroundings?

3. Skeeter presents a challenge to Sarah when her pouty behavior belies her cuteness. What are some of the pitfalls that loom when you take on someone else's children for the long or short term?

4. Living in the country presents opportunities and obstacles. Brett learns to embrace the opportunity of the farm and Sarah's way of life. Liv yearns for town, for people, for things to do. Which do you prefer, city or country? Why?

5. As Craig recognizes his growing affection for Sarah, he sees their families as roadblocks instead of seeing their romantic relationship as a building block to bridge family problems. How often do we see the glass as half-empty rather than half-full?

6. Craig's initial perception of Sarah is of someone monotoned and reserved, with little affect. When he glimpses a hint of her inner turmoil after the roadside encounter with Brett and Liv, his opinion begins to change. How does clinging to our perceptions impede our spiritual and emotional growth?

7. Sarah's attempt to gain help from her father and half brother is unsuccessful. With no mother and a father who spurns her, Sarah chooses to draw strength from her Heavenly Father. How do our choices and behaviors affect the young people watching us daily? Do we give them the best example to emulate?

8. Sarah works hard to maintain a stoic nature despite difficult times, a trait she learned from her mother. When Craig goes out of his way to be nice to her, she doesn't know how to react. Can you think of times when a gentle demeanor offset anger or defused a volatile situation?

9. When Brett finds Craig at the Water Flow, Craig realizes the boy needs the influence of a good man and he steps into that role. Is it reasonable to expect a gentle hand of leadership can turn a life around, make a difference in this day and age?

10. Craig faces his Rubicon when he must leave an injured Sarah to fend for herself and wrestle her own insecurities. As a take-charge man and a healer, this goes against his grain. How difficult is it to trust those we love to God, to walk away when we're convinced we know better?

11. Craig admits to himself that if he'd known Sarah's farm lay across the road from his building lot, he probably wouldn't have bought it. He gives God the credit for seeing down a road Craig couldn't discern. Has God ever opened doors for you without you recognizing it at the time?

12. When Craig asks Brett to join him at a widely attended town function, he knows he must inform his grandmother. To his surprise, his step forward opens doors for Rita's return to town life. How often do our actions spur a ripple effect among others, where good inspires more good?

13. Proximity thrusts Craig and Sarah together although they've never actually dated. How important is proximity to a relationship and what can couples do to promote proximity during today's busy lifestyles?

TITLES AVAILABLE NEXT MONTH

Available July 27, 2010

LARGER-PRINT BOOKS!

GET 2 FREE
LARGER-PRINT NOVELS
PLUS 2 FREE
MYSTERY GIFTS

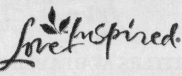

Larger-print novels are now available...

HARLEQUIN®

A Romance

FOR EVERY MOOD™

Spotlight on

Heart & Home

Heartwarming romances
where love can happen
right when you least expect it.

See the next page to enjoy a sneak peek
from Harlequin® American Romance®,
a Heart and Home series.

*Five hunky Texas single fathers—five stories from
Cathy Gillen Thacker's* LONE STAR DADS *miniseries.
Here's an excerpt from the latest,* THE MOMMY PROPOSAL
from Harlequin American Romance.

"I hear you work miracles," Nate Hutchinson drawled. Brooke Mitchell had just stepped into his lavishly appointed office in downtown Fort Worth, Texas.

"Sometimes, I do." Brooke smiled and took the sexy financier's hand in hers, shook it briefly.

"Good." Nate looked her straight in the eye. "Because I'm in need of a home makeover—fast. The son of an old friend is coming to live with me."

She was still tingling from the feel of his warm palm. "Temporarily or permanently?"

"If all goes according to plan, I'll adopt Landry by summer's end."

Brooke had heard the founder of Nate Hutchinson Financial Services was eligible, wealthy and generous to a fault. She hadn't known he was in the market for a family, but she supposed she shouldn't be surprised. But Brooke had figured a man as successful and handsome as Nate would want one the old-fashioned way. *Not that this was any of her business…*

"So what's the child like?" she asked crisply, trying not to think how the marine-blue of Nate's dress shirt deepened the hue of his eyes.

"I don't know." Nate took a seat behind his massive antique mahogany desk. He relaxed against the smooth leather of the chair. "I've never met him."

"Yet you've invited this kid to live with you permanently?"

"It's complicated. But I'm sure it's going to be fine."

Obviously Nate Hutchinson knew as little about teenage

boys as he did about decorating. But that wasn't her problem.
Finding a way to do the assignment without getting the least
bit emotionally involved was.

*Find out how a young boy brings Nate and Brooke
together in THE MOMMY PROPOSAL,
coming August 2010 from Harlequin American Romance.*

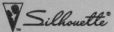